A Little Family Business

Anne Louise Bannon

HH
Healcroft House, Publishers
Altadena, California

Contents

ISBN 978-1-948616-25-6

Library of Congress Control Number: 2022909285

Healcroft House, Publishers, Altadena, California, United States of America

To my own little family, Michael Holland and Corrie Klarner. None of us has the same last name, either

Acknowledgments

Can I just simply thank every human being I have ever known for their help, both hidden and seen?

I suppose not. Still, family has been a consistent theme in my work, so I must thank my parents, David and Connie Bannon, and my siblings, David Bannon, Jr., and Lori Bannon, for laying that all-important foundation. I have to thank my daughter's father, Gary Klarner, for giving me a wonderful daughter.

But then there is my own immediate nuclear family that we formed when I married my husband, Michael Holland, and brought into that marriage, my daughter, Corrie Klarner. When I first wrote A Little Family Business, back in the early 1980s, Corrie was not even the proverbial twinkle in her father's eye. I had no idea then that I would get divorced and have to stitch together a step-family. But that experience did inform in the subsequent re-writes how Sid and Lisa begin to form their little family.

Finally, I want to offer a shout out to Meredith Taylor for her insights on dealing with a grieving child, not to mention my good friends Carol Louise Wilde, Jane Rollins, Kirsten Hansen, Michael Starch, and a cast of thousands. You all enrich my life immeasurably.

July 24-27, 1985

I knew that meeting was not a good idea. I told upline that it was not a good idea. But they needed somebody nobody would ever suspect of being an operative to meet with Cat's Cradle. A youth group leader supervising a church camp outing? Who would suspect her of being an operative with an ultra-top-secret organization under the auspices of the FBI? And yet, I was both of those things.

Every year, during the last full week of July, my church hosts a week-long retreat for our teens at a Christian camp on Catalina Island, which is around twenty-five miles off the coast of Los Angeles. I'm one of the leaders. On Wednesdays, we hiked into Avalon, the main city on Catalina, spent a few hours letting the teens run around and hopefully, not get into trouble, then got on a boat or two back to the camp about two or three inlets north of the town. My Quickline superiors thought what a terrific opportunity. I did not agree, but I was stuck.

I had no idea what the meeting was for. I did not have Need to Know. That was one part of the whole espionage culture that truly peeved me. I mean, I get that espionage is based on secrecy. But it had happened more than once that Sid Hackbirn, my partner, and I had been told we didn't have Need to Know only to find that if we had known, things would have been a lot safer for us and resolved a lot more easily. It didn't matter. Someone over me had decided that I didn't have Need to Know, so I wasn't going to be told squat.

Needless to say, I was not in a good mood that Wednesday morning as we campers and leaders gathered near the beach to begin the hike. I'd volunteered with my friend Kathy Deiner to make sure the cabins were clear. I managed to get on the side where my cabin was and slid inside long enough to get my Smith and Wesson Model Thirteen revolver hidden in my daypack. However self-absorbed your average teen girl is, it would have been too hard to get the gun out of my suitcase and into the pack without being seen if the girls in my cabin had been there. And I sure as heck wasn't going unarmed. I suppose it would have been easier to keep the gun in my daypack from the get-go, but I used the pack for too many other things besides toting armor and it might have been noticed.

I checked the rest of the cabins, which were clear, and hurried down to the beach. The first part of the trip was hiking up into the hills and scrub of the island. Now, I love to hike, and I was probably one of the few people in the group who thought it was actually fun to walk up the steep trail and over the switchbacks until we walked down the slope into Avalon.

The next challenge was to get away from everybody and find the narrow alley where the meeting was to take place. As the teens and leaders gathered around the sack lunches the camp staff had brought to the pier near the beach, I slid away. The sandwich wouldn't have been enough to feed me, anyway. [Nothing is enough to feed you, my darling locust. - SEH]

In the alley, the man was there. He was balding and his face ash colored.

"Cat's Cradle?" I asked. "I'm Little Red.

He nodded, then groaned.

"Take this," he gasped, and shoved a piece of paper into my hand. "Get it to—"

I realized he was holding his side and blood seeped between the fingers of his hand. He crumpled. His head flopped back, and his eyes suddenly began staring, utterly unseeing. My stomach lurched, but I held it down and did what any normal person would do. I screamed bloody murder. As the crowd gathered, I faded into it, then ran like crazy for a pay phone. Sadly, the last thing I could do was stay and get interviewed by the police as a witness.

I found one at the back of a restaurant that I knew my friends liked. I dialed the phone card number and Sid's pager, then hung up, and looked at the paper I'd been given.

A minute later, the phone rang, and I grabbed it.

"Hello?" I asked.

"Hey," he said. "How did the meeting go?"

"It didn't," I said, trying not to cry. "He was wounded, shoved a piece of paper at me, then died."

"Oh, honey," Sid sighed soothingly.

"At least, I didn't barf."

"That's an improvement."

"I still feel terrible. He's dead."

"I'm so sorry you have to deal with it, lover." He paused. "Have you looked at the paper yet?"

"Yeah. There's some sort of code on it, but I can't figure it out. I haven't had a chance and don't have much time before someone begins to wonder where I am. I told them this was a bad idea."

"I know. I agree. Listen, I'll call upline with the news. How's your week been otherwise?"

We talked for several more minutes about what all had been going on since the previous Saturday when I'd left, and generally complained about not being together. Then I saw Kathy Deiner at the front of the restaurant looking around.

"They're looking for me," I grumbled. "I'd better get going."

"Okay. I'll see you Saturday."

"See you then. I love you."

"I love you, too."

"There you are, Lisa," Kathy said, coming up. She's a tall woman with close-cropped hair, rich chocolate skin, and a completely elegant demeanor. "Where have you been?"

I glanced at the pay phone and decided to tell her part of the truth. "I went to call Sid." I made a face. "I miss him."

"Oh, Lisa." She patted my shoulder, then grinned. "I'll bet you do."

Sid doesn't go to camp with me because he's an atheist.

"Let's go get something to eat," I said, trying to shake off the emotions roiling my stomach.

"Sure. Why not? Dan is never going to get all those kids rounded up to meet the boat back early."

"What? We've got a couple hours, at least."

Kathy sighed. "There was a murder over in an alley not far from here. Didn't you hear the screaming?"

"No," I lied. "How terrible. What happened?"

"I don't know." Kathy shrugged sadly.

I crossed myself. We found Father John in the front of the restaurant on the Avalon boardwalk and he asked us to join him. I wasn't sure where Kathy's husband, Jesse, was, although he usually stayed moving and took lots of pictures of the teens, photography being his passion as well as his career.

John is a tall man with salt and pepper hair and solemn brown eyes. He's the pastor at the Catholic church I go to, and the one responsible for me being involved with the teens. He is also my confessor and one of the very few people who know what Sid and I really do when we're not being freelance writers for magazines.

As Kathy and I slid into the booth on the patio, I could see Dan and Sarah Williams having what looked like a disagreement on the sidewalk.

"He's still not going to get those kids rounded up anytime soon." Kathy picked up a menu. "And I don't see why he should."

John made a face. "A man was killed."

"I know." Kathy's brows knit together in pure pain. "And I don't want to be callous, but there isn't any connection to us. We just happened to be in the same place at the wrong time."

John glanced at me, and I forced my face into a blank. Kathy didn't notice.

"Darn it, John," she continued. "You know we've got parents already upset because the camp is run by a bunch of fundamentalists. We do not need to give them any more reason to complain."

"True." John shifted. "But that is my problem, not yours."

"If it weren't for Dan..." Kathy grumbled.

Dan Williams is our youth minister, and while he is devoted to the kids, he can be a little on the conservative and controlling side. The problem is that a lot of the parents in our parish are fairly progressive. Dan's fundamentalist bent doesn't always play well with them, and some of those parents are really vocal and controlling, themselves.

A nice young waitress in a blue Hawaiian shirt ran up to our table and waited expectantly.

Kathy looked around. "Think I can get away with getting a glass of wine?"

A little over half the camp leadership was militantly dry and camp rules forbade alcohol except for sacramental purposes, so those of us who liked the occasional drink tended not to flaunt it when we were there.

"Probably not," John half-smiled. "On the other hand, there just might be some rum in my cola."

"Lisa?"

I swallowed. "Rum and cola it is. And I think I'll have the chili burger, too."

We put in our orders and watched as three of the teens went running past. Another four girls had rented a pedal car together.

John said something but was drowned out by the roar of a sea plane with bright red stripes along the side taking off from the bay on the other side of the boardwalk. Fat drops of waters splattered everywhere outside as the plane soared over us, seemingly close enough to graze the roof of the restaurant.

"What did you say?" Kathy asked John.

"I was just wondering what Lisa thought about the incident."

John's eyes focused on me. I shrugged slightly, feeling guilty even though I knew I wasn't. I couldn't help feeling as if I'd brought the killer to the island because of that meeting. I hadn't told John about it, but he'd obviously noticed that I'd split off by myself pretty quickly.

"I'm kind of with Kathy on this one," I said, wincing. "We should probably pray for the victim, but I think the less attention drawn to the incident, the better."

John's eyebrows rose briefly upward. Kathy, thank God, didn't notice.

"Let's see what the kids are saying when we get back," he said, shifting a little.

After lunch, Kathy and I went shopping. Avalon is mostly about the tourist kitsch, and Kathy and I are not. But we frequently find some unusual goodies. I found this cute pair of backless sandals with carved wood high heels and soles and bought them. Kathy bought a really cute sarong-style skirt. We didn't buy anything else but looking at all the t-shirts and mugs helped take the edge off my nerves, which were still jangling even if I wasn't acting like they were.

As we all had expected, the kids were fully wired when we got back to camp, but that had little to do with the murder in the alley, thank God. It was actually normal for Wednesdays. One of the goals that we camp leaders had was to jolt the little stinkers out of their usual self-absorption into compassion and caring. Nonetheless, that day I found that same self-absorption a saving grace. I got the feeling that Dan sort of thought so as well.

Dan did insist on an all-camp tug of war, which helped settle the kids down a bit before dinner. John took a couple minutes to check in with me, and I told him part of what had happened, and reassured him that nobody had noticed me, nor were there any bad guys coming back to camp.

As we finished eating, Frank got up and did mail call. I wasn't expecting any letters. The previous two years at camp, Sid had sent me at least one, plus a postcard of questionable propriety each year from where he'd been vacationing in the Bahamas. He wasn't in the Bahamas that year. He was in Newport Beach, California, with my sister Mae, her husband Neil, their five kids, and Sid's son, Nick. I'd gotten Sid's letter the day before.

"Oh, I have one final postcard," Frank announced happily. There were a few cheers. Several of the kids were repeat campers. "I don't know, Lisa. I think your business partner has lost his edge. There isn't one innuendo on this card. It just says, 'With love.'"

There were several boos.

"On the other hand, it is from Las Vegas and there's a picture of an Elvis impersonator on it."

I laughed. It was an ongoing joke that Sid and I had to stave off nosy questions about when the wedding was going to happen. We told people several things, but our favorite was that we had gone to Vegas and gotten married by an Elvis impersonator. The kids cheered happily.

As for Sid, he hadn't lost his edge. He and Frank's best buddy, Esther Nguyen, could turn the air blue with their ribaldry in a New York second. However, what Sid had lost was his appetite for sleeping around and had only recently promised me his fidelity. Our commitment to each other was very solid.

Later that night, we had the big prayer service we always did on Wednesday evenings.

"This is a special chance to make a real commitment to the faith that you've been baptized in," John told us. "Most of us were baptized as infants, a choice our parents made in our names. That doesn't change what the Sacrament did for us. Sacrament is the tangible expression of the spiritual reality. But there does come a time when each of us must make a choice whether or not to live that reality. Some of you have made that choice already. Here's a chance to pray for the deepening of your baptismal sacrament and pray for where God is leading you. For others, it's an opportunity to make a commitment to living your baptismal sacrament."

During the next part of the service, we leaders prayed with individual kids. As I prayed, my hands on various kids' shoulders, in the back of my mind, all I could think about was that poor man who'd died that day and Sid.

Sid got the concept of commitment, and he always had. He simply hadn't believed in marriage because he'd been taught that it was a crock, and he'd seen enough failures in that arena not to question what he'd been taught. Still, he didn't mind marrying me.

It had shocked both of us, but I was the one who was having trouble with the idea of being married. My fears were centered on all the social expectations, which was why I had wanted to remain single. But then Sid came along, and we fell in love, and when you fall in love you're supposed to get married, and I just couldn't figure out what to do about that.

Marriage is a sacrament in the Catholic Church, and what John had said about sacrament got under my skin. It was one of those things that I thought Sid would never get (and to a degree, he didn't). But it was important to me. I couldn't say why or how, but it was.

Being confronted yet again by Death that day only added the urgency to my thinking. After all, Sid's and my work could be quite dangerous, and we both had learned not to leave things unsaid or unresolved. We never knew if we'd have another chance to say or resolve them.

So, I made the decision I did later that night. I'd had this nightmare that I get when I'm stressed out. I'm sure it had been triggered by the murder earlier that day. For the first time since the previous spring, Sid was not there at my side. Yet, I could almost feel him next to me, his hand rubbing my back, his soft voice soothing me. He was part of me. I made up my mind, then pulled the decision out multiple times over the next few days and prayed over it.

Saturday was the day we all went home. There was always a bittersweetness to the end of camp. For most of the kids there, it was pretty emotional. Some had their first experience of real faith, some got a better grip on who they really were, a couple would literally turn their lives around. I knew one kid that year who was leaving a place of safety to go back to a truly ugly situation at home. Still, even with the emotions, most of us had had a perfectly wonderful time and would cherish those memories but were eager to get back home to the people we loved.

As the boat home docked in Long Beach, I knew Sid would be there with the other parents who had volunteered to drive the campers back to the church parking lot. He'd helped drive us down the week before, too. I got a good grip on my suitcase, sleeping bag, and daypack and left the boat, searching among the other adults on the quay. We saw each other at the same time.

Sid is not a large man, barely three inches taller than me and I'm average. He has dark, wavy hair, a cleft chin, and gorgeous, gorgeous blue eyes. The second I got onto the quay, he was there. I dropped my luggage and we kissed each other hungrily, with Sid's hand sliding into the back pocket of my shorts.

"Hey, you two!" One of the parents nudged us. "There had better be a wedding happening soon."

"Maybe we're already married." I grinned and looked at Sid.

We both rolled our eyes. Then Sid patted my upper arm and I yelped.

"Again?" he asked.

Okay, I frequently forgot to put on sunscreen, and it was the third year running that I'd come back from camp with a sunburn.

"I was only going to be out five minutes. Then one of the kids wanted to confess."

That was the other interesting part of camp. Since the topic of my talk was "Sex and the Problem of Temptation," when somebody wanted to talk about his or her lapse that way, they came to me, and it was seldom a short conversation.

Sarah Williams ran past. "Sid, how many?"

"I have room for three."

This was the absolute worst part of the week for Sarah. She was terrified that a kid would be left behind and scurried around with her lists, checking and double checking, and woe to the parent that left without her say so. We had never left anybody, but that was probably because Sarah was so careful.

"Okay, Leslie, Gina, and Brittany!" Sarah made a note. "Go with Sid and Lisa! Sid, do not even think about leaving until I say so."

"That's really him!" Gina gasped as the three girls lugged their suitcases and sleeping bags to the space next to us.

"Yes!" Brittany screeched. They were all three fifteen. "And we've got 'em!"

"What?" Sid looked at me.

"The Talk," I said. Sid's prior randy behavior was a significant part of the talk. Well, he had offered himself as a bad example that first year. "My darling, you are infamous, you know."

Many of the teens were getting used to seeing Sid around and had met him. But Gina was new that year.

Sid laughed. "Good afternoon, ladies."

"Hi, Sid," said Leslie, also giggling.

When Sarah had everybody grouped by carload, she began dismissing us. Our carload was in the middle of the pack.

The girls chattered incessantly about their week and everything else in their worlds. Sid and I kept our hands to ourselves since any time Sid looked in his rear-view mirror, or at me, or I looked at him, it brought on gales of giggles. There may have been four or five cars that left ahead of us, but our car got to the church first, thanks to Sid's lead foot. Other parents were there waiting, and barbecues had been set up to feed the campers when they arrived. I verified that Leslie, Brittany, and Gina all had their families there and helped unload their luggage. Then I said goodbye.

"Aren't you going to stay for the barbecue?" Leslie's mom asked.

"Uh, no. We're going to head out." I said with a smile. "Thanks, anyway."

I got back in the car.

"You sure you don't want to stay long enough for a snack?" Sid asked, starting the car.

"No. I want to see Nick."

The next day, Sid's son, Nick, would be heading home to the Bay Area where he lived with his mom. That night we were going to celebrate my niece Janey's ninth birthday.

"So, what's been going on?" I settled into my seat.

"Rock Hudson announced that he has AIDS on Thursday." Sid's face looked a little grim.

"What? Heterosexual contact?"

Which, granted, was probably not the way most people reacted. But Sid and I had a different take on that. One of his former girlfriends had gotten AIDS, although she'd probably gotten it from a drug addict she'd met after sleeping with Sid. Sid's first test had come back negative, but since his last sexual contact had only been that past spring, it was always possible that he'd picked it up from someone else and his doctor wanted him to assume he could spread it until he was tested again in October.

"No. Hudson's gay."

"Huh. I didn't know that."

Sid shrugged.

"Actually, I was wondering more about whether you got any more information on that meeting from Wednesday." I looked out the windows as Sid pulled onto the 405 freeway.

"Not much. Cat's Cradle was from Division Thirty-Four-Alpha."

"Deep undercover investigations."

As in, so deep undercover, you were there for life.

"Yeah. Henry's going to try to find out what he was working on." Sid slowed as the traffic slowed near the airport.

"Anything else?"

"No. It's been a nice quiet week. I did get your letters and thank you."

"Thank you for mine. And the kids liked the post card. So, did you guys have fun?"

"We've had a great time." Then Sid frowned. "Something's really up with Nick, though. He swears he's not being molested, and I believe him, but whatever's been bothering him is getting worse. He absolutely refuses to talk about it, too. Even threw it in my face that we have something we can't talk about to him."

"What's Mae been calling it? The onset of adolescence."

Nick and my nephew Darby were both twelve at the time, and both were getting a little mouthy.

"It's more than that." Sid shook his head, keeping his eyes on the road ahead.

"Well, do we want to put him in counseling?"

"If we could keep him down here long enough. You know how he's been this past month or two. Wants to come down, then goes right back up. I was shocked that he agreed to stay the whole week here. Said his mom wanted him to come. And he's called his mom every single day."

"He's never done that before."

"The only good thing was that I was able to tell him that we'd find a way to take care of him." Traffic had loosened up and Sid pressed the accelerator.

"That's what we discussed." I glared at the freeway ahead. "Have you been able to talk to Rachel at all?"

Rachel was Nick's mother.

"She absolutely refuses to talk to me."

"Have you tried talking to Marlou?"

We had figured that Rachel's friend Marlou was in on whatever was going on.

"Yesterday. She said she understood, but there really wasn't anything she could do about it, and that Nick was happy that we'd agreed to take care of him."

"We're going to have to take custody, aren't we?"

Sid sighed. "I don't see how we can avoid it. But maybe we can push it off until the house is done."

Sid wanted to take custody of his son. We both did. Only there was our little side business. Neither of us thought we could keep it secret from Nick, but dumping something like that on him, not to mention, the danger we were often in. It just didn't seem right or fair to Nick.

We arrived at the beach house shortly afterward. The house was crowded and noisy with kids yelling. Nick was in the bedroom he was sharing with Sid and Darby, talking to his mother. Darby came down for a quick hug, then went right back upstairs. Janey, brown-haired, hazel-eyed, came up and tried whispering in my ear.

"What?" I asked.

"Uncle Sid bought us Cheetos and ate some!"

Sid laughed and hugged her. "You silly girl."

"Cheetos, huh?" I laughed.

Sid rolled his eyes as Janey ran off. We both knew she'd been behind the Cheetos. Sid is totally down on junk food but can't really refuse when Janey asks. I was a little surprised that he'd eaten some, too, but not entirely.

The twins, Marty and Mitch, who were almost five, burst into the room roaring like engines. They bumped into me, got their hugs, and went back to tearing around the beach house like little red-headed cars.

Ellen, age seven, came running up with a clear plastic box with a bright turquoise lid. "Aunt Lisa, we went to the tide pools and look what I found!"

I wasn't sure what was in the box, but it didn't matter. "That's very interesting."

Mae hugged me and I went through the small living room that opened out onto a patio that opened onto the walkway that stretched along the land side of the beach. Neil was there, grilling chicken breasts for dinner. I gave him a hug, then Mae and I settled onto the couch in the living room. Sid got a couple bottles of beer from the fridge and brought one to Neil. Mae handed me a glass of cold white wine.

"So how was your week?" I asked her. I could hear Darby practicing his violin upstairs.

"We've had a terrific time. Oh, let me show you some of the photos. I already got them developed." Mae pulled out a stack of prints. "I had so much fun with your camera. Thank you for loaning it to me. That zoom lens was a blast."

I looked at the print of Darby, Neil, Sid, and Nick sitting on the short wall between the walkway and the sand. All four of them had their eyes glued to the backside of a bikini-clad young woman. I laughed.

Mae laughed, too. "I got that from the balcony upstairs."

"What's this?" It was a photo of Sid with the older kids gathered around him. He was dressed in his Hawaiian print swim shorts and had the matching shirt over it, but open, and he was sitting on a bicycle. "I don't think I've ever seen Sid on a bike."

"That's because before this week, Sid didn't know how to ride one." Mae giggled. "He'd never learned. Janey wormed it out of him when he kept dancing around it when the kids wanted to rent bikes and have him go riding with them. That's them teaching him."

Sure enough, in the next picture, Sid was wobbling. In later shots, he sailed along as perfectly cool as ever.

"Lisa!" Nick burst into the room and tackled me.

"Hey, how's my sweet guy?" I hugged him back and kissed the side of his head for good measure.

"Careful, Nick," Mae groaned. "You're going to knock over the wine."

"It's okay, Aunt Mae." Nick plopped down next to me. "I'm so glad to see you!"

"I'm glad to see you."

And I was. I adore Nick. He's sweet and bouncy and bright and looks just like his dad, only Nick wears glasses and has longer hair, with a lock that constantly falls over his forehead.

That's when Neil called us to eat dinner. We had cake and sang to Janey, and she opened her presents. As the sun started to set, I gently pulled Sid away to walk with me down to the water's edge.

"Cheetos?" I asked as we trudged through the sand.

Sid sighed and looked heaven-ward. "It was Janey's idea."

"No, duh." I laughed. "And...?"

"Okay." He shuddered then shrugged. "Time to confess. I used to have a junk food habit and I loved Cheetos."

"Past tense re the Cheetos?" I grinned at him.

"Eh, maybe still present tense." His eyes glittered in the dark. "And why do I get the feeling that you know about that?"

"Your former junk food habit? Conchetta told me about it when I found the cans of Dr. Pepper in the pantry."

"That, too." Sid swore. "I can't do any of that anymore. You do understand, don't you?"

"Yes, I do."

The waves roared and Sid's eyes glinted in the starlight.

"So, why did you pull me out here?" he asked, smiling.

"I have something I'd like to talk to you about and I didn't want to do it in the car." I faced him and put my hands on his chest, then took a deep breath. "I want to get married. In the church."

Sid's eyebrows rose. "Are you sure? I mean, that's been a pretty scary thing for you."

"I know." I bit my lip. "I am going to keep my name. But it was that bad pickup. We see so much horrible stuff, and then John was talking about living our sacraments." I shrugged. "It's like you say. My faith is the glue that holds me together, and after that bad pickup, I kept thinking that we could use that extra glue, I guess. I want us to have that."

"Fine. Sure." Sid gave my shoulders a quick squeeze.

"Are you okay with it?"

Sid laughed. "I don't care either way. I made my promise to you. That's what counts to me."

"It does to me, too. It just would be nice to have the sacrament, as well."

"Then we'll have it." He paused. "Are we going to do a whole wedding?"

"I'd like to, sort of." I frowned, then smiled. "It would be really nice to celebrate our life together with the people we love."

Sid thought about it for a second. "You know, it would be. Let's do it."

"And if anybody gets obnoxious about it, I'll cancel it and we'll just have you, me, and Father John." I looked back at the beach house. "We should probably tell the family while we're all here."

"Let's do it tomorrow morning. I don't want to steal Janey's thunder."

I was shaking as I leaned my forehead against the bridge of his nose. "So. We're getting married."

"Yeah." Sid sounded bemused. "We are."

July 28–29, 1985

One of the reasons Sid had rented the beach house for the week I was at Catalina and had the O'Malleys join him was that all of us were in the process of moving, sort of. Sid and I were just remodeling but given the drastic changes we were making to the place in Beverly Hills, we'd had to move out temporarily to the condo across from the one belonging to Kathy and her husband, Jesse.

We'd bought the condo in early May, while the architect was still pulling permits for the job on the house. Sid's independently wealthy, thanks to an inheritance from presumably one of his relatives, so we can do stuff like that. Paying cash means that escrow goes extra quickly, and by mid-June, we were crammed into the two-bedroom condo. We'd decided to donate a lot of the furniture from the house, but our books, records, tapes, art, my fabrics, Sid's baby grand piano, sheet music, most of the files, those were all in storage.

Mae and Neil, on the other hand, were moving. Neil had gotten a post as an associate professor of dentistry at the University of Southern California and would start that fall. So, he'd sold his practice in Orange County. They sold the house in Fullerton right around the same time as we'd bought the condo. They'd decided to settle in Pasadena, where Neil was able to start a part-time practice since he was expected to keep one even though he was teaching full-time. They also found a house in the northern part of the city that, well, was not in the best of shape. It had been built in the early teens and it had really good bones, but it needed a lot of work. With escrow on the house in Fullerton taking its sweet time, then the escrow on the Pasadena place also moving at a snail's pace, it wasn't until July that everything closed and suddenly Mae and Neil had two weeks to pack up five kids and nine years of stuff only to find that the house that they were moving to needed to be completely re-plumbed and re-wired.

Mae was so freaked out that when Sid offered to help out with the extra costs, she accepted. So, we paid for a rental place in the area, plus the movers, and storage for what couldn't go into the rental place. After all, Mae and Neil were going to be spending a lot of money on renovations. We'd spent most of the two weeks before camp, sorting, packing, and donating. Mae remained beyond frazzled, which is why Sid called in a favor and somehow got the beach house, never mind that those places are usually booked months, if not years, in advance. The Saturday I left for camp, Mae and Neil supervised the movers and turned over the keys to the old house to the agent. I'm not sure where they stayed that night, but the rental was from Sunday to Sunday, and apparently, the week had made a huge difference in Mae.

Sid made breakfast that Sunday morning, whole wheat banana pancakes, with a little bit of raw sugar to go on top. Right before he put the pancakes on the griddle, we went into the room where he'd been sleeping and called my parents to let them know about getting married.

How everyone else in the condo did not hear my mother's scream of jubilation, I do not know. My ears were ringing, though. Daddy wasn't as thrilled, but then he was just barely getting used to Sid. It wasn't Sid, oddly enough. Daddy does like him. It's just a lot like he's still getting used to Neil, if you know what I mean.

"Now, do you have your date yet?" Mama asked.

"Um. We're still kind of getting used to the idea," I said looking frantically at Sid.

"Well, that's the first thing you have to do, honey. Oh, I am so excited! You're happy this time, right?"

"Yes, Mama. I really am."

"Oh, good. Welcome to the family, Sid."

"Thanks, Althea."

"Now, I'll need to get together a list."

I took a deep breath. "Mama, we want to keep this small."

"Of course, Lisle, baby."

"Mama, if you try to make a big deal out of this, I swear I'm going to cancel everything, and it will be just us and the priest. I mean it."

"Oh. Well, you're right. Can I be a little bit excited about planning the wedding? I've been waiting so long."

I laughed softly. "Sure, Mama. I'll call you as soon as we have a date."

Sid laughed, kissed my nose, then went downstairs to start cooking pancakes.

As we finished eating, Sid cleared his throat loudly. The others quieted. I took a deep breath.

"Okay, everyone." I swallowed and looked at Sid. "Sid and I have decided to get married."

"No, duh," said Darby.

"You're copping out, Dad," Nick said, but he had a big, happy grin on his face.

Everyone else was cheering and congratulating us, and I was still trying to catch my breath.

"Oh, look at me. I'm shaking." I looked over at Sid.

"Why, Aunt Lisa?" Mitch asked.

I blinked and smiled at him. "Because we just made the decision last night and I'm still in shock."

Sid laughed and squeezed me. "I think we both are."

"We're so happy for you," Mae said, blinking, too.

"Then why are you crying, Mommy?" Marty asked.

"These are happy tears," Mae said. "Sometimes, you just get so happy, you cry."

Sid got up. "Okay, kids, I'll need some help cleaning the kitchen, and then we need to make sure everything's packed. I have to have the keys to the rental office by noon."

Janey and Nick went to help Sid in the kitchen. Darby gave Mae a little bit of attitude but went to the room he was sharing with Nick and Sid and started packing. Mae was everywhere at once, trying get sheets off the beds, dusting, and cleaning.

"I'd better get these into the washer," she called, her arms filled with sheets.

"Mae, you don't have to do that," Neil said.

"Oh, my god, look at all this sand! Janey and Ellen, come help sweep this up."

"Mae!" Sid yelled at her. "The rental company said not to worry about the sand. There's a cleaning service coming, and they'll take care of cleaning everything up. They have to, anyway."

I took the sheets from her. "Come on, Mae. We'll put these on your bed, then we'll check and make sure nothing gets left behind."

"Okay." Mae looked at me and began weeping again. "You're getting married. I'm so happy for you, Lisa."

"Thanks."

Soon we were all on the sidewalk in front of the house, and Sid was locking the door.

"Sid, I can't thank you enough," Mae said, giving him a big hug. "I cannot tell you how much we needed this week."

"More than happy to."

Then the O'Malley family got into their van and Nick, Sid, and I got into the Beemer. Sid dropped the keys off at the rental office in plenty of time. We headed back up the freeway to LAX to drop Nick off for his flight, stopping somewhere near Hawthorne to get lunch and kill a little time.

"Hey, Dad, do you guys know when you want to have the wedding?" Nick fidgeted with a French fry.

"I'm not sure," said Sid.

"It won't be for a while yet," I said. "We're getting married in the church, and that takes some time to set up."

Nick looked relieved. "Good. I was hoping you weren't going to go running off to Vegas right away." He grinned. "Can I be in the wedding?"

"Sure, Nick." Sid looked a little shocked, then smiled. "You're part of this, too. Why don't you be my best man?"

"Cool!" Nick sat up suddenly and looked at Sid and me. "Wow. We're going to be a real family, aren't we?"

"You have your family with your mom," Sid said.

He looked so sad all of a sudden. "Yeah. I do." Then he brightened. "But we'll be a family, too."

I looked at Sid, my heart fluttering. "Yeah."

We got Nick onto his plane, and Sid called Marlou from the airport to let her know. In the car, it was clear that he was annoyed, and I knew darned well why.

"We agreed not to make any promises about taking custody," Sid said after we'd pulled onto the freeway.

"I didn't. He's right. We are a family now."

Sid glared at me, but he wasn't quite ready to give up. "Yeah, well, try telling Nick you didn't mean taking custody when you agreed that we are."

"Try telling Nick you didn't mean taking custody when you told him we'd take care of him no matter what."

Sid grunted. He hates it when I deflate a good snit with logic. [And you like it when I do the same to you? - SEH]

"But what if we can't take custody, Lisa?"

"Then we'll figure it out. Just like we've been doing."

He shook his head. "Why does everything have to feel like we're making it up on the fly?"

"Probably because we are."

"I just wish I knew what game Rachel is playing. It would make it a hell of a lot easier to make a decision."

"But then life would be easy, and that would be no fun at all."

Sid started breaking up but forced himself to keep his eyes on the road.

"No, it wouldn't," he said. He smiled softly as he shook his head. "I can't help thinking how lucky I am to have you."

"And I'm lucky to have you."

"But it brings to mind our conversation last night. I forgot to ask you something."

I looked over at him. "What?"

"Crunchy or air-puffed?"

"Huh?"

Sid glanced over at me and grinned. "It's the ultimate test of compatibility. Crunchy Cheetos or air-puffed?"

"Crunchy. Duh." I laughed.

"Whew!" His eyes flitted my way again. "Have I told you today how much I love you?"

"Actually, no, you haven't."

"I think when we get home, I'm going to have to show you."

I couldn't help shifting as the excitement ran through me.

Yes, I am Catholic, and I do believe that sex belongs in the context of marriage. But I also believe, and always have, that being inflexible when it comes to the rules can be more harmful than sticking to them no matter what. Sid had been raised with the belief that free love was a good and healthy thing and that marriage was a lie. He had bent far enough to promise me fidelity and a lifetime commitment. What kind of person would I be if I weren't willing to bend on what defined marriage?

However, the reason we weren't having sex yet was because of the possibility that Sid had picked up the AIDS virus. Sid wasn't about to trust condoms. He had a point. He'd been wearing one when Nick was conceived. He was worried enough that he might have infected me through our saliva. [We didn't know yet that wasn't possible. - SEH] By the time we'd discovered he'd been exposed, it was way too late on the saliva thing, so that was the only bodily fluid of his that he would let me near.

And yet, that night...

When we got to the condo, I unpacked. I cleared my daypack, stuffing the bits of paper into my purse, then stashed the daypack and my sleeping bag in the closet in Nick's room. Sid made dinner out of the freezer and pantry and still managed to tease me at the same time. After we'd eaten and cleaned up, we started necking on the couch that we'd brought from our living room at the house. We were doing all the things I tell the teens not to do, with the important distinction being that Sid and I were adults in a committed relationship.

Sid's hands began wandering and then so did mine. We'd been getting pretty free with our hands since May, but always outside our clothes because Sid was being really careful about the bodily fluids thing. That night, Sid really leaned into it. He moaned happily, then suddenly yelped, gasped, and got up.

"Did I do something wrong?" I asked.

"Something right, but..." He gasped again. "I'll be back in a minute."

He hurried off to the master bedroom. I followed him. He'd gone into the bathroom there but had shut the door.

"Is everything okay?" I asked after knocking on the door.

"It's fine. I'm just undressing." Sid was usually modest around me, not because he cared if I saw him naked or not, but because I tended to freak about that sort of thing.

I bit my lip. All of a sudden, my curiosity overwhelmed me.

"Do you mind if I come in anyway?" I asked.

He laughed loudly. "Sure. Come on in."

I was a little embarrassed to find that I'd made him, um, happier than I'd thought.

"I'm sorry," I said.

He laughed again. "You have nothing to be sorry for. It felt great. It's just a bit of a mess is all."

He finished getting undressed, tossed his clothes into the hamper, then bent to pick up an errant sock.

"Your butt's all hairy."

That also made him laugh. "Most men's are, my innocent one."

Then I saw something else. "Sid, that scar on your left side? Is that a bullet hole?"

"Yeah." He chuckled. "I usually tell people it was a jealous husband, but it was actually me being stupid. I had the suspect bound around a pole next to a desk but had left the suspect's gun too close. Caught me there right before the Code Nine team came in to make the arrest. They were not happy. It's funny now, but it wasn't then."

I kissed my fingers, then touched the scar. He gasped happily. Then he turned and faced me.

"Well, here, I am." He smiled softly.

He is very nicely assembled. However, what really caught my notice were the other scars. He had a white-ish strip on his left bicep. I remembered when a bullet had grazed him. We hadn't been able to go to the hospital to get it stitched up.

Then I saw the thin white line under his left nipple. I'd seen it before but hadn't asked.

"Knife?" I asked, gently touching it.

He nodded. "The suspect wasn't too happy about being cornered."

I kissed the little, almost invisible line, then the stripe on his left arm.

Which led to me asking questions about what sex is really like because I'd only been wondering my entire life. So, Sid put on a pair of jeans to keep me safe from his bodily fluids, then offered to demonstrate on me. That meant first undressing me and getting to look at me fully naked for the first time. He'd seen my breasts a couple times, although he still swears that first time was an accident. [It was. A happy one, but an accident. - SEH] He also kissed the knife scar on my left arm, which I'd gotten the summer before, and the other knife scar just under the hairline on my forehead, and the burn scar behind my right ear.

The result of the demonstration was mind-blowing and kind of left me wondering if I still qualified for taming unicorns, and not caring at the same time because it was so good and delicious and amazing, and besides, the unicorn is a mythical beast. We tried a couple more experiments, which were not only a lot of fun, but equally intense for both of us. Then Sid said we could share the bed, which was his old waterbed from the house. We'd been taking turns sleeping on the couch while the other took the bed because Sid was finding it a little on the physically painful side to sleep next to me and not make love. Apparently, we'd found a way to relieve that little problem. I sighed happily as he snuggled up to me.

"Thank you," I said.

He chuckled. "For what?"

"For tonight. For making me feel so good."

"Oh."

I frowned. "Did I say something wrong?"

"Not at all." He held me closer. "I've just never had anyone thank me before."

"Seriously? You've got to be kidding. Never?"

"Well, praise and some appreciation here and there, but straight-up gratitude? No."

"You poor thing." I reached around and kissed him. "Well, I am grateful. And I want you to know it."

He smiled, his gorgeous eyes shining. "You're very welcome. And thank you. You made me feel very good, too."

I rolled back over and fell asleep with him curled around me, nuzzling my ear.

[That night was something else. I'd always known you to be a very passionate woman, no matter how tightly you kept it in check. Even apart from the personal feelings that were developing, I knew that once I found the way to unleash that passion, sex with you was going to be a whole new level of intense. That night, I first saw just how badly I'd underestimated you. Add the love we had for each other, and let's just say you rattled my back teeth, it was so good. Then you thanked me, and you still do every time we make love. You have no idea how much that means to me. - SEH]

The next morning, Sid nudged me awake. We put on our running shorts and shoes, and I put on my bra and t-shirt, and Sid put on his muscle shirt. We ran for our usual hour. The building we were in was in that section of Wilshire Boulevard called condo canyon because of all the high-rise apartments and condos there. Our building sat on a corner with a much smaller side street. Sid and I generally left the place through the side entrance. We ran up one side of Wilshire and down the other.

When we got back, Sid decided to shower in Nick's bathroom, while I showered in the master bath. After I dried off, I looked at myself in the mirror over one of the two sinks and noticed the masking tape I'd placed on it two days before I'd left for camp, when my period had started. Of course, I was done by that time, so, I was a little late doing my breast self-exam. I didn't want to skip it, though. I took the tape off the mirror and tossed it.

As I raised my arm to begin, Sid knocked on the door.

"Mind if I come in?" he asked. "My shaving stuff is in here."

"Sure." I began palpating.

Sid got his shaving brush, ran some water in the second sink, and started foaming up the shaving soap. He had on his undershirt and silk boxer shorts. I spotted him looking at me as he lathered the lower part of his face. I moved to my other breast. I figured he knew what I was doing.

"Why don't you shave in the shower?" I muttered. I gave my breasts one final visual inspection.

"Can't see what I'm doing in the shower." Sid carefully scraped around the dimple in his chin.

His face was barely inches away from the mirror, so I knew he hadn't put in his contact lenses yet. He's very nearsighted. His contacts case and wetting solutions sat on the counter between the sinks, next to the rack with our toothbrushes in it, and my mascara, blush, and lipstick.

I pulled the toothpaste and floss from the drawer in the cabinet, and my own deodorant. I flossed, then brushed my teeth. Sid wiped the remaining soap from his face and checked out his chin and cheeks.

I yawned. "How is that I am standing here buck naked next to you in your skivvies, and I am not freaking out?"

"I have no idea." Sid laughed softly. "But I like it.

He reached out, hesitated a second, then squeezed my backside. I squeezed his, then headed into the bedroom to get dressed. We were even using the same tube of toothpaste, for crying out loud.

I could hear the whine of the blow dryer in the bathroom as I stared at the contents of my closet. There was a closet in the bathroom and one in the bedroom. Neither was larger than the other, so I'm not sure why I'd gotten the one in the bedroom and Sid had gotten the one in the bathroom. We'd also picked up a lovely antique dresser, which was in the bedroom, and we each had a set of drawers in it. I decided it was too hot for nylons and pulled from the closet a short-sleeved linen jacket, a full skirt in a pretty print, and a white tank top. Then I got dressed and put on a pair of wedge sandals. As I went back to the bathroom to fluff out my hair and put on what little makeup I wore, Sid came out in his slacks and shirt, his tie for the day draped around his neck, and carrying his suit coat and vest. In the bathroom, I put my makeup on, looked at myself in the mirror again, shook my head, and turned to the bedroom to put on some earrings, my watch, the chain with Sid's class ring on it, and my promise ring.

We had never done anything like that before. Well, we did share the bathroom, but not at the same time. In fact, Sid was almost always very modest around me, and even then, I'd still get embarrassed. And yet, that morning, it was so... Ordinary. As I left the bathroom, Sid slid into his suit coat. He was happy, but he looked as bemused as I felt.

"Are you awake enough to talk?" he asked.

"Maybe. Why?" I am not a morning person.

"Well, we'll probably have to go out to get breakfast. The milk went bad, and there wasn't that much, anyway. There's no fruit, either."

"Oh. Okay."

Sid slid his pocket watch into its vest pocket and looped the chain around one of the buttons. "Before we do, though. Um, I just thought we might want to call the rectory. See if we can get a time to set up our date."

"Huh?"

"I was thinking we might as well face the music and get it taken care of." Sid smiled at me. "This is our life now."

I thought it over. "Yeah. I guess it is. It is nice."

"I thought so."

We got in to see Father John just after nine that morning. John took one look at us as we came into his cluttered office, grinned, got up from his desk and gave us both a big hug.

"Let me guess," he said, releasing us. "Are you two here for a sacramental purpose?"

"Sacramental exactly," I said.

"As in, we're doing it," Sid said with a rueful smile.

"Let me get the book. Have a seat." Laughing, John went out to the front office, got the wedding book from the secretary, then came back in and settled himself behind the desk. "I have to say, it's about time you two came to your right senses."

Sid shifted in his chair. "Well, this is more about Lisa's religion thing."

"Like hell." John laughed even louder. "I mean, I'm glad you're going for the wedding. But, come on, Sid. The two of you have been in love forever. It's past time you went public with it. Alright. Let's see what's open."

Our first opening was the first of March, the following year. We picked noon for the time and John wrote us in, then went over all the different paperwork, suggested signing up for an Engaged Encounter weekend as soon as possible for the pre-Cana classes, given that our schedule was prone to changing unpredictably. Then John closed the book and looked at us.

"I don't usually discuss this with couples. Most don't give a damn. A few aren't going to do anything. But it is my job to point out, that according to the rules, sexual intercourse outside of marriage is still a no-no."

Sid rolled his eyes. "That's not even going to be an issue until October at the soonest."

"Is that your next test?" John asked. He watched Sid nod. John knew about our little situation. "However, while heavy petting is frowned upon because it can lead to sexual intercourse, between a couple preparing to be married, it is not condemned. That's the official line. I, personally, have a real hard time seeing it as a sin when two people who love each other deeply and are committed to each other, when they follow through on that physically, even before the wedding. Lisa, if and when you feel like you are in a state of sin, I do want you to talk to me. And, Sid, if you have any questions, you know you can talk to me, as well."

Sid nodded. "I know, John, and I appreciate it."

I was in a good mood when we left. Sid wasn't.

"You okay?" I asked him as we headed to the grocery store and the mailbox place to pick up our mail.

We'd been using a private mailbox for years, which made things that much easier when we moved from the condo.

"I'm just worried you're going to feel guilty if we do engage in full intercourse in October." He winced. "I was really looking forward to it."

"I don't think I will." I shrugged. "On the other hand, we just got a free pass on last night's activities."

"How?"

"Heavy petting, Sid." I shifted as I thought about it. "It's not condemned."

Sid laughed and shifted himself.

Once we got home and got lunch together, I called Mama with the date and agreed to spend that Thursday looking at reception sites with her. After all, that needed to be done first, and soon, or it would be too hard to find a spot.

"I'll have to put her up in a hotel, too," I told Sid. "We don't have any room here."

"Fine. We've got two acceptances and three rejections."

"Okay." I pulled out the padded leather three-ring binder Sid had gotten for us to help keep everything organized.

I was doing well with my tickler file, but it was nice having one place where I could keep track of everything, including appointments, stories, addresses, all cross-referenced to each other. We were just finishing the mail when our Quickline pagers went off.

"It's my turn," said Sid. He picked up the phone.

We were in the condo's living room with both our desks jammed up against each other near the couch. The second bedroom was Nick's, and we only used the bathroom next to it for the second shower. The dining table from the house was in the dining area next to the tiny kitchen. My two sewing machines took up roughly two-thirds of the dining table and an ironing board was set up next to the wall. The other third of the table was where we ate. On the other side of the door to Nick's room was a blank wall and we'd put an upright piano there. Next to that was a tiny utility room. The walls were bare, and the curtains industrial. But it would serve until the house was finished.

Sid made the pickup that had come in while I concentrated on getting the writing work organized and getting a rough draft done. That night, I went to the Teen Bible Study with Kathy and her husband, Jesse. It was kind of a follow-up to camp, with warm emotions overflowing. Then I talked Kathy and Jesse into going to Jefferson's for a drink and invited Esther and Frank along. They were a little surprised to see Sid there, at first. But then all four looked at the two of us and realized what was coming.

"I'm so happy for you!" Kathy gave me a big hug.

Esther looked at Sid and laughed. "You really going to get married in church?"

"That's the plan," Sid said, reaching over to take my hand. "I'm starting to look forward to it."

July 30–August 4, 1985

In spite of being newly engaged and, um, sharing the bed full-time, it actually felt like a fairly quiet week. Monday's pick up was more information about Cat's Cradle. He had apparently located an arms dump of stolen U.S. weapons and was trying to get that information to his colleague, Player Piano. Player Piano had gone silent, however, which meant either dead or deeply hiding. Sid got the feeling that we'd get tagged to find him or her. We looked at the piece of paper that I'd gotten from Cat's Cradle, but it was just a series of numbers. Sid made a copy, then sent the original upline to a code specialist we knew in San Francisco.

Tuesday, Conchetta Ramirez, our housekeeper and cook, came by to clean and to bring us our mail and our three cats and Motley, my liver-colored springer spaniel, whom she'd been babysitting, along with the two cats belonging to Jesse and Kathy. Conchetta is in her mid-forties, with black hair sporting several silver hairs throughout. She mostly wears jeans and concert t-shirts from hard rock bands. Long John Silver is a one-eyed gray short hair and had given birth to four kittens the previous fall. Sid and I had kept two, Fritz, a gray tabby, and Blueberry, a fluffy female so gray she looks blue. Jesse and Kathy had adopted the two black and white kittens, Viola and Chin-Chin.

Conchetta was only coming by two days a week, since there really wasn't that much to keep clean and Sid is pretty neat, anyway. The cats were not happy. At the house, our three were indoor/outdoor cats, and at the condo they had to stay inside all the time. We weren't sure which one did it, but one of them expressed profound displeasure by pooping in one of Sid's favorite dress shoes. We put out litter boxes everywhere. Motley was simply happy to see us and begged for walk after walk.

Jesse came over from across the hall to return Fritz who had gotten out and offered to walk Motley again for us. Jesse, a photographer, is a little taller than Kathy with cocoa-color skin and his hair in a round cut. Kathy still worked as an accountant. They had inherited their condo from Jesse's former roommate, George Hernandez, along with George's substantial assets, so neither technically needed to work, but they did, anyway.

The four of us had gotten into the habit of walking across the hall and into each other's place for lunch or occasionally just to chit chat, especially in the evenings. Several times a week, we ate dinner together, too. Kathy and Jesse's place is larger than ours, with an extra bedroom and a deeper living and dining room. They also don't have sewing stuff all over their dining room table. They were my primary ride to church. Since parking was a premium at the building, my truck had been put into storage at the garage where Sid kept his beloved, but retired, Mercedes 450SL.

While Jesse was walking Motley, Sid and I talked Henry James, our immediate supervisor, and his secretary Angelique Carter, into coming to an early dinner with us. They met us, along with Henry's wife, Lydia, and we told them about the wedding. Henry is a public information officer for the local FBI office. No one else knows that he's also a floater operative for our part of Quickline. Henry, Lydia, and Angelique are good friends with us. Angelique was ecstatic, which relieved me no end. She'd been in love with Sid for a long time, but eventually realized that wasn't going to happen and gave him up.

Henry just laughed and shook his head.

"You were right, Sid," he said, chuckling. "It was only a matter of time."

Sid laughed. "Well, you were right, too, Henry."

I had no idea what that meant, but let it go.

That night, Sid joined me at the end of the Single Adults Bible Study, made up of mostly recently married adults, to announce that there was going to be one less single person in the group. I also made it clear that the second someone got anywhere near out of hand, that I was going to cancel the wedding. That seemed to stave off Janet Weinstock and Sylvia Perez, who were wedding-crazy and did not get that not everyone felt the same.

On Wednesday, Jesse, Kathy, Sid, and I concluded at dinner that night that maybe just walking into each other's place was not a good idea. This was after Jesse walked in on us just as Sid had gotten under my skirt. Jesse and I were both humiliated. Sid didn't see what the big deal was. Kathy thought it was hysterical. I was glad we hadn't gotten too far in the proceedings, as I remembered that in the bad old days before Sid gave up other women, he was not prone to stopping what he was doing just because someone else showed up in the room. I was also annoyed, although it hadn't been Jesse's fault. It had been my idea for Sid to get under my skirt. The four of us agreed that knocking and waiting for an answer was a good idea.

I had been dreading my mother's visit, but I have to say, it turned out to be a good one. We saw several places that looked promising and that had openings. But it didn't go entirely smoothly.

"Have you even started your guest list?" Mama asked me at lunch that day.

"I tried to yesterday afternoon but got distracted."

"Well, honey, we have to have an idea of what people you want to invite so we know how big a space we need."

"Can we limit it to fifty people?"

Mama laughed. "Lisle, baby, that will barely cover our relatives."

"But they're in Florida. They won't want to come all the way out here."

"Oh, yes, they will. Some of them are already making plans."

"Do we have to?" I blinked back tears.

"I'm afraid so. They'll never let me hear the end of it."

"Maybe I should cancel the wedding."

Mama looked worried. "You're still going to get married, aren't you?"

"Oh, of course. We just won't have a wedding."

"Well, if you think that canceling the wedding will shut your relatives up, you can think again. They'll probably be even more tiresome."

"Okay. We'll figure something out."

I must admit, once Mama and I stopped by the condo to pick up Sid so that we could go out to eat, I was almost excited about things. We went in the side entrance, as usual, but Mama called Sid from the lobby and asked him to bring down the address book. He did as he was requested. Then, at the restaurant, Mama sweet talked him into putting together the initial guest list. He finally started showing some interest. We had just over one hundred names by the time we were done, though fortunately, that included my aunts and uncles. I did get to put my foot down on inviting cousins.

"You know, Sid," Mama said, putting her hand on his arm. "When Lisle told me that you had asked Nick to be your best man, I thought that was the sweetest thing ever."

"He's pretty special, Althea," Sid said, and I could have sworn he swelled with a touch of pride.

"He is such a darling. Just like his daddy."

I smiled, relieved that my parents were ready to accept Nick as one of their own.

[Seriously? Lisa, you and I had just been played by a true master. I love your mother. She is the kindest, sweetest human being I have ever met, besides you, and I'm sure she meant what she said about Nick. Still, I remember some months later, it had to have been Christmas, when she twisted my arm into calling her Mama. Neil saw me standing shell-shocked and clapped me on the back.

"Mama got you, didn't she?"

"Yeah."

"There's a reason we love her daughters."

"I'm afraid so." - SEH]

Later that night, as Sid and I cuddled before going to sleep, I had to ask.

"How are you doing?"

He shook his head. "I'll be fine. Your mother was right. We needed to get the guest list taken care of. Now, you two can take care of the site and everything else your mother wants."

"I'm not doing everything her way."

"I know, Lisa. It'll work out."

The next morning, I drove Mama to Pasadena, where she, Mae, and I were going to have lunch.

"You okay, Lisle?" Mama asked.

I shrugged. "Good enough."

"Lisa! Be careful!"

I was driving Sid's Beemer and dodging around cars. Truth be told, more than one car chase has had its effect on my driving habits.

"I am careful," I said.

"You never used to drive this way. Anyway, what's bothering you?"

"Sid's just not as interested in the wedding as he was last night."

"Oh, honey. You can't expect much more than that. He is a man, after all."

"Sid's not your average man."

"I'll give you that. But I have never met a man who was interested in weddings. He's probably just trying to figure out what it means to be married and all that. You've said how many times he was raised to believe it was a crock. Change like that isn't easy for anybody."

The problem was, Mama was right. Sid probably was having some trouble adjusting to the idea of being married. Lord knows, I was having trouble with it, too.

We met Mae at a restaurant, and she was bubbling over with news about the kids and the house. I let it all wash over me, then drove back to Los Angeles.

Sid got me out the next day to go antiquing. One of the problems we'd had over the previous few months had been that Sid had suddenly found himself with all sorts of time on his hands. He'd been going out to chase women four to six nights a week, and often all day and night on Saturdays. So, what was he supposed to do instead? He'd been cooking dinner more often, one advantage to being out of the house. Dinners with Kathy and Jesse had also helped. Then there was the house. We'd gotten rid of a lot of things when we'd moved out, including the everyday pottery ware and the fine china. But that meant we needed to replace it, and I needed to be there because part of the whole reason we were remodeling was to make the house more our house, rather than Sid's.

I didn't mind too much, until Sid got into extended discussions with the various dealers on provenance and signature marks and other stuff that made no sense to me and bored me to tears. Still, it was better than trying to finish a sewing project with him looking at me balefully. He felt about fabric roughly the same way I felt about watermarks.

That Sunday, Kathy needed to get to church extra early to talk to the nine o'clock mass about the parish festival that was coming up in September.

"Is it that time already?" I asked.

"I'm afraid so. Do you mind?"

We left the house around nine-thirty, which would get us to church around quarter 'til ten. Kathy wouldn't be doing her pitch for volunteers until near the end of mass, when the announcements were read. She and I were both scheduled to serve at the ten-thirty mass, I as a Eucharistic minister, Kathy as a lector. Jesse stayed in the assembly. Kathy and I were chatting in the sacristy behind the altar about ten minutes before mass was due to start when Sid poked his head into the room and waved at me. I was startled but went over to him.

"What's going on?"

"Nick called right after you left. Rachel's in the hospital. We've got to go up to Sunnyvale now."

"What's going on?"

"I'll tell you in the cab."

I looked back at the group of ministers and the priest who would be saying mass. He was a visitor who showed up about once a month or so. Kathy saw us and came over.

"I've got to leave," I told her. "It's an emergency. Can you guys take care of the animals, please?"

"Sure. What's going on?" She looked at both Sid and me.

"Something with Nick," Sid said. "We'll call you once we know what it is."

"Oh, dear Jesus," Kathy replied, crossing herself. "We'll pray for you. Take care."

I ran after Sid to the cab that was waiting. We'd barely settled ourselves in the back when the driver pulled out.

"What's happening?" I asked Sid.

He closed his eyes, then opened them again. "Rachel's game. She's been sick this entire time."

"What?"

"She has leukemia. She was diagnosed in January last year, right before she brought Nick to us. According to Nick, she was confident she could beat it, but wanted to find his father just in case."

"Why didn't Nick say anything?"

"She swore him to secrecy. She didn't want anybody to know. Not her colleagues at the hospital, not her family, and especially, not us." Sid trembled.

"That witch!" I snapped.

"Lisa, she's also dying. That's why Nick has been so anxious to get home these past couple months. He wants to be with her."

"But to dump a secret like that on her own kid?" I groaned. "How could she?"

"I know. On the other hand…"

Sid looked at me and I nodded. If Nick could keep a secret like that, he could keep our secret. I desperately hated the thought of dumping that on him, but it did make it possible for us to take custody.

"Oh, no," I said. "That's why he's been so worried about the custody thing."

Sid nodded. "No doubt." He paused. "So, are we?"

"He's your son."

"You're just as involved as I am."

I swallowed. "What do you think?"

"We should be able to pull it off." Sid stared straight ahead. "But I'm not doing it without you."

I put my hand on his knee. "We'll do it, then. You know how much I love Nick."

Sid smiled softly and put his hand on mine. "Thank you, Lisa. You have no idea how much I appreciate that."

We didn't say much on the flight up to San Jose airport. Once there, Sid rented a car and got a map and directions to the care facility where Rachel was. When we found the room, Nick sat at his mother's side, watching her. Marlou Parks, a small, moderately round woman with brown hair and bags under her eyes, sat nearby on the bed's other side. Rachel lay on her back in a still sleep I'd seen in people during their last days. I had brought the Eucharist to several families keeping that fearful watch. Most times, it was sad, but still the peaceful winding down of a long, fruitful life. Occasionally, it was a life ebbing away far too soon. I closed my eyes.

"Nick," Sid said softly.

He bounced up. "Dad!"

He ran up and hugged Sid hard.

"I told you we'd get here as fast as we could." Sid held him back.

"Lisa!" His voice filled with tears as he held me. "I'm so glad you're here."

"Nicholas," whispered Rachel's weak voice, so unlike the formidable woman I'd met before. "Who's here?"

Sid went over to the side of the bed. "It's Sid and Lisa, Rachel. We're here and we'll take custody of Nick when the time comes."

She half-smiled. "Thanks."

"I wish we'd known."

"I didn't want you to take my boy too soon." Rachel swallowed. "Nicholas, take your father and his girlfriend to our house and get them settled in."

"Mom." Nick frowned.

"You can come back."

Marlou looked up. "I'll be here, Nicholas. You take care of your dad and Lisa, and then you can come right back."

Nick looked downcast but nodded.

"Nicholas," Rachel whispered. "I love you, baby."

"I love you, Mom." He kissed her cheek and held her hand with that special gentleness I often saw in his father.

I held him close to me as we left the room and went to the rental car.

I hugged him extra tight right before putting him in the back seat. "Oh, my poor baby."

"I'll be alright," Nick said glumly. "It's just waiting, you know? Each time I leave, I think it's going to be the last time I see her."

Sid put his hand on Nick's back. "I'm so sorry, Nick. We'll be here as long as you need us, and then you'll come home with us."

"You mean that, Dad?" Nick looked up at him.

"Yes, I do. So does Lisa."

"I do, Nick. We're here and we'll be with you all the way."

He hugged me again, then got into the car. When we got to their house, Nick insisted on helping with Sid's and my luggage, dropping it only to unlock the front door.

"Marlou's been staying in my mom's room," he explained, as he let us inside.

"Where do you want us to stay?" Sid asked.

"I don't know."

"Why don't you show us upstairs?" I said. "Then we can figure out what to do."

There was a guest room, and Nick's room featured a bunk bed. I motioned to Sid, and he nodded.

"Nick, do you mind if I stay in your room?" Sid said.

"What about Lisa?"

"I can stay in the guest room," I said. "Sid, can you help me with my suitcase?"

Sid looked a touch puzzled but agreed. Once we were alone, I turned to him.

"How are you doing?"

He shrugged. "Feeling a little out of my element but managing. I can't think what Nick is going through."

"I know. It's going to be hard for him, but he'll be okay. He looked pretty relieved when you said we were taking custody."

Sid nodded. We went back to Nick's room. He had opened Sid's carryon bag and was sitting on his lower bunk, looking at a billfold with a pained look on his face. In his other hand, he held Sid's Model Thirteen revolver. My heart stopped.

"Dad, what is this?"

"Nick, put the gun down."

"No! Not 'til you tell me what this is!"

"I will tell you when you put the gun down. I promise."

Nick's face was creased with pain, but he laid the gun down on the bed. Sid crossed the room and got the gun into the shield that got it past the airport metal detectors, then stashed it back into the carryon.

"Dad!" Nick waved the billfold. "This is an FBI ID, but it's got your picture on it and some name, Charles Deverux."

"Devereaux," said Sid quietly.

He looked up at me. We'd wanted to wait to explain to Nick. He was going through enough. I shrugged. It couldn't be helped.

"And here's Lisa, only it says Linda Dever-whatever."

"Dever-oh," Sid said. He took a deep breath. "It's what we couldn't talk to you about, Nick. Why I was worried about taking custody of you."

I sat down next to him. "Nick, we are taking custody. We will take care of you. But those IDs make things pretty tricky for all of us."

Nick looked at me. "Why?"

"The last thing we wanted to dump on you, especially now," I said. "It's our secret."

Sid sat down on his other side. "Nick, within the structure of the FBI, there are several smaller organizations so top secret only their members know they exist. Lisa and I are part of one."

"Which one?" His face took on an anxious frown.

Sid shook his head. "I'm afraid it's a pain in the butt known as Need to Know. As in you do not Need to Know."

I put my arm around his shoulders. "Nick, we cannot tell anyone we do this. My family does not know. Aunt Mae, Uncle Neil, my mom and dad, they have no clue, and they can't know because it would put theirs and our lives in danger." I played with the lock of hair that had, once again, fallen over his forehead. "You've been carrying around an awful secret these past eighteen months, and it's killing me and your dad that we must ask you to keep another. But you must. Do you understand?"

Nick took a couple deep breaths. "I hate secrets."

"I know, Nick," I said. "I hate them, too. But sometimes they are necessary. You don't have to hide anything from us, and we will be here to support you, and love you, and take care of you."

"And maybe even train you," Sid said.

I glared at him, but he was right. Nick would probably need to learn the skills we depended on to keep ourselves alive.

"Train me?"

"If you know about us, you're part of the team," Sid said.

Nick closed his eyes and reached over to Sid. The two of us just held the boy for several minutes.

The sound of the front door opening and closing immediately put Sid and I on alert. Nick looked scared for a second.

"Someone's come in," he said.

Sid put his finger to his lips. He nodded at me, then slid out of the room to investigate. A moment later, he returned, his face heavy.

"It's Marlou," he said.

Nick looked up at his father and knew. Slowly, he broke down in sobs.

August 5-13, 1985

The next few days went by in a blur. There was so much to do, and poor Nick's heart was so heavy.

Rachel had brought Nick to meet Sid in February 1984. But late the prior fall, in November 1983, Rachel's mother had died suddenly of a heart attack. Sid and I had good reason to believe that Nick's grandmother had been the one primarily raising him, and the two had been close. For Nick to lose his mother only a year and a half later must have been utterly overwhelming.

There were phone calls to be made. Jesse agreed to continue taking care of our cats and Motley. He also offered to pick up our mail and send it overnight to us every couple of days, along with some of the files that we were working on. I hated asking for the files, but the truth was, Sid and I still had deadlines to stay on top of. Mae, when I called her, was properly scandalized at Rachel forcing Nick to keep her illness secret. I bit back my response because I didn't want to say anything bad about Rachel when Nick could possibly hear. I also felt guilty about making Nick keep Sid's and my secret, but it couldn't be helped.

Sid was really nervous about calling Henry but needed to let Henry know that we were going to be out of town for however long. He did not want to tell Henry that we were taking custody of Nick.

"You're going to have to," I told him the day after Rachel had died. "How are you going to hide it from him that Nick's around all the time?"

Sid sighed. "I know. I just do not want to get put on Code Five status. Crap, that's boring work." He paused. "But Nick is more important."

I got on the extension while Sid made the call.

Henry got on. "Hello, Benedick, the married man."

It was a joke I had made, based on the play Much Ado About Nothing.

Sid cleared his throat. "Henry, there's a problem."

"What?" Henry's voice immediately became serious.

"Lisa and I are going to be stuck in Sunnyvale for several days. I'm not sure how many."

"Sunnyvale. That's where Nick lives, isn't it? Are you trying to get custody of him?"

Sid growled. "No. I am taking custody. I don't really have much choice. His mother passed away yesterday."

"I'm so sorry, Sid. That must be rough on him."

"It is. We still have that case with Cat's Cradle to work, though."

"Yeah. You're going to need to check in with Blue Shield. Wait, she's up in the Bay Area. You can do it while you're there."

"But what about Nick?" Sid sounded really confused, and in truth, so was I.

"What about him?"

"Aren't you going to put us on Code Five status or something?"

Henry laughed. "I couldn't if I wanted to."

"But he's a kid."

"Sid, I raised my two boys working this business. I know of at least three people in our line whose spouses and kids have no idea what they really do. Yeah, you're right to be concerned. I spent a lot of time worrying that my kids would accidentally give me away, that someone would come after them, that I wouldn't be there for them. But people fall in love and create children. These things happen. Just tell Nick as little as possible. He's old enough to keep his mouth shut."

"And you can get it cleared upline?"

"It's been cleared. We set it up when Nick first showed, just in case." Henry sighed. "Let me guess, you've been agonizing about it all this time."

"We both have. Bringing a kid into this business…"

"It's scary. But I do wish you'd said something sooner. I could have reassured you, and I probably would have told you to wait to take custody until you had to. Well, you have to now. It won't be easy, but you'll figure it out. Let me know what's going on when you talk to Blue Shield, okay? And… I'm sorry to hear about Rachel. I know you two had some problems, but it can't be easy."

"No, it's not."

They hung up and I met Sid on the stairs.

"That went well," I said.

"A lot better than I thought." Sid let his breath out. "Alright. What's next?"

We needed groceries - there was next to no food in the house. There were more phone calls to be made, not to mention arrangements for the funeral, plus all the legal work, decisions to be made about what to do about the house, and when Nick would be ready to move. Rachel's friends kept calling, in shock because they'd had no idea she was sick, let alone that sick.

Sid made a point of calling Whiteman, his lawyer, then faxed the will and Rachel's other papers to him from the local copy store while we were out for groceries.

Then there were Rachel's two brothers. She also had a sister, but the sister had the decency not to descend on us Monday afternoon assuming that Rachel's affairs were a mess. Her brothers were not only peeved because they were convinced they would have to clean up whatever mess had been left behind (never mind that there wasn't one), both had a glint of greed in their eyes as they looked over the living room. Marlou almost collapsed, but Sid just quietly informed them that Rachel's affairs were perfectly in order, which they were, thank God, and sent them on their way.

Rachel's will clearly gave Sid custody of Nick, with the bulk of her assets going to her son. Nick and Marlou were to split any profit from the house, however. Marlou had been designated the executor and had been given decision making power over the house, the funeral, and a few other things. The problem was Marlou had been Rachel's primary caregiver since the end of the previous May, as well as taking care of Nick since early that spring, and the poor woman was completely exhausted, not to mention grieving the loss of her dearest friend.

Sid, because he is that kind of man, took up the burden, making sure to always defer to Marlou. I almost got a little jealous of Marlou, but I do know one thing about Sid and that it is he is kind and caring above all else. It's one of the things that I love about him.

For my part, I focused on the writing and being close to Nick. The kid was devastated, but at the same time, a little relieved. It had been insanely hard watching his mother decline, and I could see there was part of him that was grateful that it was over, even if he didn't realize it.

Wednesday morning, over breakfast, the pagers went off. Neither Nick nor Marlou noticed because the pagers only vibrated but Sid and I looked at each other.

"I'll get it," I mouthed, then said out loud. "To heck with fruit. I think we need donuts. Anybody have any favorites?"

"What's that one with the swirls on the side?" Nick asked. "I like the ones with chocolate on the top."

"French crullers," I said. "I will do my darnedest to find you some."

Sid gave me half a glare. He is big on the whole health food thing. I'm not. Nick wasn't enthused about the health food thing, either. I'd seen a donut shop not far from the housing complex where Rachel's house was and went there first. I bought four crullers with chocolate on top and a couple bear claws for me. Okay. I eat like a horse and can get away with it somehow. It's one of those things that baffles Sid, because he can't. I did wait to eat the bear claws until after I'd found a pay phone and called in. I pronounced the caller code, she gave the receiver code.

"What's up?" I asked.

"I need to set up a meeting with Big Red," she said. "I'm told you're here in the Bay Area."

"Blue Shield?"

"Yeah." She sounded vaguely surprised.

I saw a diner down the street and set up a meeting for lunch at twelve-thirty there. She was happy to meet me.

Sid was not enthused but agreed we couldn't really refuse. The big problem was Nick.

"What do you mean you're leaving?" the boy cried, his face dissolving into terror.

I glanced at Sid. "I'll have the meeting. You can stay with your dad outside."

"I can come with you?" Nick's face lightened.

"Of course, son," Sid said.

Poor Nick. He didn't realize that going meant an extended lecture on meeting protocols, but that's what he got. However, I was in the diner at twelve-thirty, enjoying a chicken-fried steak in a booth next to a window overlooking the sidewalk. A woman with light brown hair, neatly styled, and wearing a light-colored linen suit slid into the booth across from me. I couldn't help smiling. I'd met Blue Shield a couple of times, most memorably, when we'd both been on a case the previous fall.

"Good to see you," she said.

I grinned. "Always good to see you. I see you survived."

"You cannot know how glad I am to have gotten that transfer here," she said.

"I'm so happy for you." I smiled. "So, what have you got for us?"

"Bupkes." She handed me the piece of paper back. "I even examined the paper for invisible inks or impressions. If that string of numbers is a code, it is the most evil and contrived I have ever come across. In fact, I don't think it's a code. It could be a vehicle identification. It could be a geographic location."

My eyebrows rose. "What if it's a geographic location?"

"The problem is there's no punctuation. Without that, it's impossible to say where it refers to."

"Shavings."

Blue Shield's jaw suddenly dropped open, and I realized she was looking outside at the sidewalk. "That's..."

"Big Red," I said, slightly puzzled. "I'm Little Red."

"Oh, right." She groaned. "I always get you two confused. But wait. He's dead."

I laughed. "He most certainly is not. The cops put it out there at the behest of upline that he was. He got out okay."

Basically, Sid had escaped having his apartment blown up by an enemy, then had his cover blown by upline to distract the KGB agents in the area.

Blue Shield looked out the window again and clearly saw Nick. As I have remarked before, Nick looks a lot like his dad, even with longer hair and wearing glasses.

"You've got a kid?"

"He does. A real sweetie, too, I might add."

Blue Shield's eyes narrowed. "You know, our systems kid always said you two had a thing for each other."

I blushed. "Yeah. More than a thing. The wedding's in March."

Blue Shield laughed long and loud, then her face sobered. "Wait. How are you dealing with him, you know?"

"Sleeping around? He gave it up last spring."

"Has he been tested?"

I sighed. "Yes. And we're waiting to test again, then we'll worry about me. The reality is, he is at risk, but it's not as bad as you might think."

She shuddered. "I live in San Francisco now. I'm a lesbian and I worry about it."

I reached over and squeezed her hand. "I don't doubt. But I'm confident we'll be okay."

I wished I could have gotten her name and address. That was kind of a problem Sid and I had with our guest list. There weren't a lot of people associated with our side business that I'd want to invite, but there were a few, and I had no idea what their real names were, nor whether I should reveal Sid's and my names. Still, I was glad when she left the restaurant with me and said hello to Sid and Nick. Nick looked at us a little strangely when Blue Shield mentioned how glad she was to see Sid alive. Well, Nick didn't know what that was about and couldn't.

When we got back to Nick's house, Whiteman had finally called and left a message to call him. Sid called right away.

"Okay, we're cleared legally to take Nick home whenever we want," Sid said to me quietly after dinner, while Nick was occupied with Marlou.

"Yeah, but..." I sighed. "Sid, we'll be taking him away from everything he knows. All his friends."

"I know." Sid's voice got high and tight. "I'm just hoping like hell a quick, clean break will help. We know he wants to live with us."

"True." I closed my eyes. "Oh, shavings! I forgot to call Dr. Heilland's office to let them know we'll miss tomorrow."

"Dr. Heilland." Sid grinned. "That's it. We'll call him first thing tomorrow. We have to cancel anyway. He's gotta have something we can do."

Dr. Heilland was a psychologist that Sid and I had been seeing since the previous spring to help us deal with our respective trauma issues.

It had been helping, and one of the blessings was that Dr. Heilland had the kind of security clearance that let Sid and I talk about our side business without worrying.

Then Nick asked Sid if they could watch a movie on the VCR and Sid agreed and the two went to choose one from the huge collection of tapes in the TV room. Nick chose The Last Starfighter, which I was happy with. But I was also worried.

Nick had gotten clingy, and it was understandable. He didn't like being apart from either me or Sid, but he really didn't like being away from Sid. That, of course, meant that Sid and I had very little time to be alone together.

After the movie ended, Sid insisted that it was time for bed. He was still sleeping in Nick's room, and I supported that.

"I want to see another movie," Nick groaned.

"Nick, it's almost ten and we have to be up early tomorrow," Sid said, sounding more annoyed than the situation warranted.

The next day was the funeral.

"I don't care. I'll be okay." Nick glared at us.

"Go get ready for bed." Sid wasn't just annoyed. He was getting mad and grumpy. "I'll be up in a minute."

Nick stomped defiantly upstairs. Sid looked at me.

"We have to expect some acting out," I said, weakly. "He's probably getting into the anger phase."

Sid just grunted. Suddenly, I realized what was driving Sid's mood and it wasn't Nick's grief. In fact, I was feeling the same thing.

"I'd better get upstairs," Sid said, and left the room.

I followed and went to the guest room and got into my nightgown. I listened for the sounds of Sid and Nick getting ready for bed and sighed. Once they'd left the bathroom, I did all the usual nighttime things and went to the guest room feeling decidedly out of sorts. A half hour later, I was not even close to sleeping when Sid slid into the room.

"It's about time, but he's out," Sid said.

He had on a pair of jeans, and I had good reason to believe nothing else.

"Oh, thank God," I sighed. I patted the bed next to me. "Sid, I think I owe you an apology."

He sat down next to me and touched my face. "For what?"

"For all the times I made fun of you for getting grumpy when you were horny and stressed out and couldn't do anything about it."

"Why?"

"I think I'm beginning to know how you felt."

Sid chuckled and kissed me. "We do have to figure this one out. I do not want Nick coming between us."

"He's not going to come between us." I smiled up at Sid. "He's part of us."

"Yeah." Sid's smile was so tender and sweet. "You're right."

The ensuing session helped a lot. But Sid was right. We were going to have to figure out how to deal with our mutual desires and the reality of having Nick around full-time.

The funeral was dismal, and for me, at any rate, it wasn't that it was a secular service. My friend Rick had died the month before of AIDS and his funeral was secular and had been terribly sad, but still filled with peace or even a bit of joy.

Rachel had chosen to be cremated, which, apparently, had not gone over well with her siblings. Her friends were still trying to figure out how they'd missed the signs that she'd had cancer and given that most of them were in the health industry, you had to give them credit for their befuddlement. It did make Sid and me feel better. However, we were both so worried about Nick, it did not entirely help.

Nick handled it all reasonably well. He did cry several times, and I was glad he did. He decided not to go to the podium to talk about his mother. Rachel's brothers tried to challenge Sid about taking custody of Nick, but Sid reminded them in that tight, but scary tone of his that meant he was getting seriously angry, about the will and that Sid's name was on Nick's birth certificate as the birth father. Rachel's brothers backed off.

There was a reception at a local restaurant after the funeral, itself. That didn't last long. When we got back to the house, Marlou told us that she was going to go visit her parents in Walnut Creek, a suburb north of Oakland, but that she'd be back the next day so that we could start packing up Nick's belongings and whatever else he wanted from his soon to be former home.

It came as no surprise that emotions were running high, making the packing up a difficult and protracted process. Marlou had moved into the house that previous spring to help care for Nick, and into Rachel's room after Rachel had moved to the hospice center. After checking with Nick, we told Marlou that she could keep anything that Nick didn't want, then she could either sell or donate the rest, as soon as she was ready to deal with it. Sid also told her that she should stay at the house until it was sold because it's harder to sell an empty house.

Poor Marlou was still completely exhausted, and again, Sid had to gently help her along. We did have to get home. Besides, Nick knew he was going to have to leave, and I found it hard to believe that it was doing him any good trying to get through his grief with the reality of moving looming over him.

Nick wasn't much help, either. He'd make a few decisions, then change his mind, then make a few more, then change his mind again. Worse yet, his mood was all over the place. One minute, he'd be smiling at a fond memory, or even laughing. The next, he'd be crying. A few times he got downright surly, and Sid and I had to gently, but firmly, let him know that while we understood he was feeling angry, he was not allowed to be rude or mean.

The problem was, Nick couldn't find several things that he wanted, such as the Christmas tree ornaments (we'd found the other decorations in the attic) and several of the books he'd had as a small boy.

Marlou didn't think there was a storage unit, and Nick was pretty sure there wasn't. We did find his baby pictures, fortunately. I also got the feeling that either Rachel or her mother had thrown a lot of Nick's baby toys and clothes away, because there wasn't anything like that in the house, anywhere, even among the few boxes I'd found in the attic. Those only held some moldy men's clothes and a couple empty whiskey bottles. Nick thought the contents had probably belonged to his grandfather, who had abandoned his grandmother when Nick was just a baby.

I also had a tough time getting Nick's academic records from his prior school, let alone his medical records. It being summer, almost nobody was in the school's office, although I did finally get through and got an official transcript on Friday. His pediatrician's office was not much help at all. Because Rachel was a doctor herself, Nick told us that she seldom brought Nick in beyond getting him his vaccinations and the occasional physical. Worse yet, Nick had only seen that doctor a couple times because he'd had another doctor who had retired shortly before his grandmother had died.

We did have a small going away party at a local pizza place for Nick and his friends on Sunday afternoon. I'm glad we did. I made sure to get everyone's address and phone number so that Nick could keep in touch, but I seriously doubted they would. They weren't trying to be mean or anything. They were just twelve, which means they weren't the most sensitive beings in creation. They had no clue what Nick was dealing with and kept chattering about all the cool things they were going to do to finish out the summer and then at school, completely forgetting that Nick would no longer be part of their activities. Nick seemed to take it in stride, though. He talked about how cool his dad's place was or would be if they ever got it finished. Still, my heart ached for him.

We finished packing on Monday. Tuesday was utter chaos. The movers showed bright and early, and while Sid and I were showing them which items were going to our storage and what few were going to the condo, our pagers went off. Sid insisted on taking his turn over Nick's protests and left to find a pay phone. In the meantime, I had to supervise because Marlou had gone back to her job at the hospital where Rachel had worked as an emergency room doctor. She said she'd be back in time to get the keys from Nick.

There really wasn't that much coming down south for us, although most of Nick's bedroom was. Sid's and my belongings, and the few things Nick would need in case the movers were not as prompt as they'd promised, were already stowed in the rental car.

Sid returned with less than happy news.

"It's another meeting," he grumbled. "This time with a potential suspect. We need to set it up for tomorrow."

"Terrific," I muttered back and looked over at Nick. "What are we going to do?"

Sid winced. "Do you mind taking it? You're the better shot if it goes that way."

"You're right." I reached over and kissed him quickly. "I'll go set it up and bring back some lunch."

"We're going wired and under our alter egos," Sid added.

I gave him a brief update on where things were with the movers and slipped out.

I came back less than an hour later with hamburgers for Nick and me and a salad for Sid.

Nick's room was empty by the time Marlou arrived. She looked around, then closed her eyes for a minute.

"This is it, then," she said softly.

Sid nodded. "Marlou, Lisa and I want you to continue to be a part of Nick's life."

"Okay." Marlou gasped.

I smiled at her. "We love him so much."

"I know and I'm glad. It's what Rachel wanted, too." Marlou sniffed. "I have to admit, the way she talked about the two of you, I had my doubts. But you've both been so great."

"Thanks," Sid said. "Marlou, feel free to take your time with the house. Given the mortgage, we can't take forever, but I can spot you a few months."

"Thanks, Sid. I appreciate it." She took a deep breath, then reached out to Nick. "Come here, sweetie. Let me give you a hug."

Nick ran into her arms and sniffed.

The two just held each other for several minutes. Then Nick gave her his keys, took both mine and Sid's hands, and we walked out the door.

We went up to San Francisco, to the nice little hotel that Sid and I liked, on Powell off Union Square. Sid got us a double room, meaning we had two beds. We checked in as the Devereaux family. Sid went through all of Nick's belongings and either destroyed or hid anything that had Nick's real name on it.

"You're entering into a new life of secrecy," Sid solemnly told his son. "What keeps us safe is that no one knows who we really are."

"So, what's our son's name?" I asked.

"Do I need one?" Nick asked. "You keep saying we're not supposed to use each other's names when you're working."

"We're undercover," Sid said. "And when you're undercover, nine times out of ten, what will trip you up are those little details. It would look pretty funny if we didn't know the name of our own son."

We both looked at Nick and grinned.

"Don't I get to pick?" he asked.

"Parents generally name their kids," Sid said.

"Why don't we give him veto power?" I said.

We settled on Ryan David Devereaux for Nick's alter ego. Nick was bemused that he finally had a middle name.

He was not happy to see Sid crawling into bed with me rather than him, but Sid whispered to me that he was going to have to get used to it. We both waited until his deep, even breathing told us he was asleep. At least, I hoped he was. It was really hard keeping things quiet enough so that we wouldn't wake him.

August 14, 1985

"Wow, Dad." Nick's voice exploded in my ear. "That thing really is hard to see."

"Stop staring at my ear." Sid's voice was softer and much tighter. "You'll attract attention."

I laughed and covered my mouth with my hand. "Coming in loud and clear."

Across the street, I saw Sid glance my way and nod. Sid and I were both wearing our transmitters and receivers. The larger part of the rigs were strapped around our waists. The earpieces sat above our ears, with a tiny tube that fed into the ear canal, and Nick was right. They were hard to see if you didn't know they were there. Of course, my hair covered my ears completely, so that wasn't even an issue.

I sat near the window of a coffee house on Geary Street. It was close to nine in the morning. Sid and Nick were across the street and went into an antique store. I thought Sid may have been buying trouble with that one, but there weren't too many other places within the range of our transmitters where one could reasonably expect to spend an hour or so. Fortunately, my contact was prompt.

Karl Mittman was a little taller than average, with blond hair, bright, blue eyes, and ramrod erect posture. It's not the nicest way to put it, but he did sort of look like a Nazi SS officer, or someone who would play one in the movies.

"Agent Devereaux?" he asked as he approached the table. "I'm Karl Mittman. I'm one of Congressman Dale O'Connor's aides. I'm so glad you could meet me today."

"How can I help you, Mr. Mittman?" I shook his hand. I was wearing a light-blue linen jacket over a flower-print straight skirt with a silk tank top underneath and wedge-heeled pumps.

"Son, set that down," said Sid's voice in my ear. "Gently."

"We suffered a devastating loss to our office a couple, three weeks ago. One of my colleagues was visiting Catalina Island and died in an accident there."

"I'm so sorry." I waited.

"Anyway, it has come to our attention that someone on your side of Justice is looking into it." He meant the U.S. Department of Justice, under whose auspices the FBI operates.

I kept my face straight. "It doesn't sound like anything in our jurisdiction. Besides, you said it was an accident. Why would anybody be looking into it?"

Mittman smiled and half-laughed. "You are aware that Congressman O'Connor is on the House Intelligence Committee?"

"So what?" I hadn't been, yet another thing someone had decided we had no Need to Know. I was fast coming to the opinion that there was plenty that we did Need to Know, and I was going to find it one way or another.

He looked around. "Let's just say we get higher levels of briefing than most committees. This seems to be coming from one of your shadow agencies."

"So? If someone is looking into it, why is that an issue for you?"

Mittman rolled his eyes. "Do I really have to explain? We just need to keep on top of things."

I shrugged and pulled a notepad out of my purse. "I'll see what I can find out for you. Victim's name?"

"Wade Acosta."

"Date he died?"

"July twenty-four. Um, local law enforcement has already checked for us, so you'll probably have to go through your higher ups."

Suddenly, the glass window next to us exploded as bullets sprayed through. Both Mittman and I were on the floor in a second. I drew my Model Thirteen revolver from the shoulder holster under my arm. A van sped away, but I got off a couple rounds anyway. It swerved and went into a traffic light on the corner.

People screamed, sirens wailed. I looked around for Mittman, but he'd gone. I debated taking off, myself, however, since I was there as an FBI agent, and since no agent would just leave, I started securing the scene. Or what I hoped constituted securing the scene. In my ear, Sid was chewing Nick out over something. Fortunately, no one was hurt, but they sure looked terrified at the gun in my hand until I waved my FBI ID around. I also holstered the gun.

"It looks like I'll be here for a while," I muttered into my top as I examined the window. "Didn't get hurt and it doesn't look like anyone else did."

"Great." Sid was not happy. "I'll take the kid down to the Wharf. Page me when you get there."

"Will do."

The cops were not happy to find an FBI agent in the middle of everything. Since I'd fired my weapon, they had me surrender it. I gave them the address of the Los Angeles office, with Henry James' name attached and hoped I'd get it back within my lifetime. The beat cops questioned me, then the detectives did. I told them the truth about who I'd been meeting, since I figured that Mittman would likely say so, and fudged about why because I could. Of course, that was assuming the cops caught up with Mittman or Mittman turned up of his own accord. I mean, it was possible that the shooting panicked him, and he ran. But it still bothered me that he'd taken off.

It was well after lunchtime when the cops said I could go. I was starving. However, instead of eating, I found a bus heading toward downtown, then got another to the Fisherman's Wharf. I was headed for one of the restaurants there when I saw Sid sitting near one of the shrimp cocktail stands at another restaurant's outside tables. Sid had dressed down, in jeans and a blue short-sleeved sport shirt with epaulets on it. Nick just wore jeans and an orange t-shirt with a Giants logo on it. The previous summer, he'd turned into quite the baseball fan. He ran around on the pavement outside the restaurant, chasing seagulls and pigeons.

Sid waved me around the half-high fence to the table and got up and held me tightly.

"Are you alright?" he gasped.

I squeezed him back. "I'm fine. It just took forever. I think I had time to pick all the bits of glass off me."

"You've still got a couple bits in your hair." Sid picked them out.

"I'm starving." I raised my hands before Sid could comment. "I know. My usual state. But I missed lunch."

"I figured." Sid pulled out a chair across from his. "You can eat, then we're getting out of here."

"Thanks."

After I had ordered, I looked over at Nick, who was still playing with the birds. "Looks like he's getting some of his normal energy back."

Sid rolled his eyes. "I keep telling myself that it's good that he is." He sighed. "How is it you can love a kid to distraction and still want to pound the living daylights out of him? Honestly, Lisa. I'm trying to listen to you, and he knows this, and he's still touching everything, and I'm trying to tell him not to without distracting you. Then, when the shooting happened, he wouldn't stay down. He wanted to see."

"He probably sees so much of that sort of thing on TV that it didn't register these were real guns."

"I just hope it registers before he gets his butt killed." Okay, Sid didn't say butt.

Nick came bounding up to the fence between the tables and the sidewalk. "Hey, Mom! See, Dad, I told you she was okay."

I winced a little at being called mom.

"I already knew that, son." Sid's smile was a little tight.

"That was cool." Nick grinned.

"No, it wasn't," I said, trembling a little. "It was scary. I didn't know where the fire was coming from. And I really hate having to draw my weapon, let alone fire it."

"Why?"

"Because I don't want to kill anybody." I blinked my eyes. "I've done it. It feels terrible."

Solemnly, Nick looked over at his father. Sid nodded.

"I have, too," he said quietly. "She's right. It's the worst feeling ever. I hope like hell you never have to feel it."

Slowly, Nick began to crumble. Somehow, I got Nick through the little half-fence and into the chair next to me and I held him. He hung on so tightly it almost took my breath away.

"Honey, I'll always be around," I whispered to him.

"I don't want you in my memories," he cried.

"Well, I don't want to be there," I said. I lifted his chin. "Your dad and I are very good at this. We wouldn't have made it this far if we weren't. Okay?"

Nick sniffed and nodded.

"That also means you have to listen to us," Sid added. "When things start blowing up, I don't have time to explain why you should do something. If one or the other of us tells you to get down, you get down and stay down. If one or the other of us tells you to stay put, you stay put."

"I'm sorry, Dad."

Sid paused. "Apology accepted."

The waitress came up with my fried clams and shrimp and French fries, all laid out on red and white checked paper. It was a good-sized platter that also held a small cup of cole slaw swimming in creamy dressing. Sid sighed when he saw it. I invited Nick to share some, and we put ketchup on the side and dug in.

"You sure you don't want some?" I asked Sid.

He put his hand up. "I'm fine."

Well, I am the type who can eat like a horse and not gain weight, not to mention my cast iron stomach. Sid needs to be more careful, both because of the calories and because his system can get pretty tetchy, especially when we're traveling. It was why he gave up his junk food habit.

As I finished, Sid announced that we were headed for the airport. Nick looked downcast.

"You feeling okay, honey?" I asked him, running my fingers through the lock of dark hair that always falls over his forehead.

"Yeah." He took a deep breath and let it out. "We have to go. You guys can't live up here, and I kinda don't want to, anyway. It just doesn't feel right without my mom."

Sid got up, then pulled Nick up from his chair and just held him. "It's a big change for all of us. But we'll make it through because we all love each other. Right?"

"Yeah." Nick looked up at him and grinned, then reached out to me.

I got up and the three of us hugged.

To Breanna, 6/23/00

Today's Topic: The Side Business

I'm willing to bet that when you came up with this idea of writing to each other to get to know each other better, you did not think we'd be tackling anything quite so heavy as last night's dinner with my parents. Frankly, I was shocked to my core when Mom told you about the side business. They almost never talk about it, even with me and I was part of it until they got put on overt status around the time I went off to college. Being known operatives does mean that they can cop to what they're doing, but they seldom do.

But it's like I wrote in our first letter. My family is intense as all get out, and it would be really hard to have an ongoing relationship with someone who couldn't handle them. It's why my relationships have all been one month and done. That's how long it took me to tell whether someone is up to handling them, and as I said last Saturday, you fit in.

Then there's also the side business. There's a good reason why my parents and I never talk about it. Keeping it a secret was how we stayed alive. Literally. But it had its effect on just about every aspect of our lives. You wrote the other day about how worried you are about the wall around me. That's the wall. It made my growing up darned unconventional and there are not a lot of people who would understand that. I'm praying you do.

Okay, so when we set up our topic, I wanted to know how you feel about my parents being counter-espionage agents and my dad killing someone the other night. I suppose I should write about how I felt when I first learned what they were. The problem is that it was all tied up with my first mother's death. I found some of Dad's equipment, and then found out my mother had died. So, when I think about that day, I don't really think about finding out about my parents.

I do know that I thought it was cool, at first. Having to keep it a secret sucked - I'll explain why later. But it did make us special. Mom and Dad also insisted that I'd have to be trained, which made me proud that they thought I could handle it. The scary shit came later.

"We need to talk about that meeting," Sid said as the plane we were on took off.

"I suppose," I grumbled. I'd been hoping for a few minutes of peace since Sid generally falls asleep as soon as the plane taxis toward the runway.

Nick sat across the aisle from us, listening to a cassette tape on the Sony Walkman Sid had given him for his birthday that year.

"Shadow agencies?" Sid asked.

I shrugged. "So what? If Congressman O'Connor is on the House Intelligence Committee, he might be privy to that kind of information."

"True, but there's also the way Mittman took off when the shooting started."

"That's the part that bothers me. He could have been simply scared, but still." I sighed. "It's nothing I can put my finger on, but something doesn't feel right about him. I hope I'm not stereotyping him just because he looks so much like a Nazi SS officer."

"Ah. That was the fellow." Sid smiled at me. "You're right. We shouldn't assume. But, my dearest, you are the only person I know who would worry about something like that."

"I hope I'm not the only one." I looked down at my hands. "Oh, shoot. Rings."

Sid and I were both wearing our wedding rings. It was a set we'd had almost since we'd known each other because we'd had to pose as a married couple more than once. Sid had a plain gold band. My rings featured a one-carat round-cut diamond. The rest of the engagement ring looked like the diamond had been set at the top of a wing of filigreed gold that curled around the main diamond, with tiny diamonds scattered throughout. The band part had a row of diamonds, although it was mostly hidden under the wing part of the engagement ring. It supposedly hooked onto the engagement ring part of the set, but I'd had no idea how since I always wore the two rings together. It was not something that I would have picked out for myself, and yet...

I'd been wearing an aquamarine dinner ring that Sid had also purchased to go with a similar necklace and earrings that he'd given me the year before. Because he'd had the dinner ring sized to the wedding set, I'd been wearing the dinner ring on my left ring finger. We called it my promise ring because he gave it to me when he promised his lifetime commitment and fidelity to me, and I promised the same to him.

"You know." Sid winced as he wriggled the wedding band off his finger. "We are eventually going to need wedding rings."

"Yes. I have my promise ring, though."

"Any reason why you can't wear both?"

"On the same finger?"

He looked at the set I'd just pulled off mine. "That probably would be a bit much. On the other hand…" He grinned. "Literally. You do have a right hand. You could keep wearing our promise ring on that one."

"Once I get it sized, yeah." I dove for my over-sized purse, which was under the seat in front of me.

Sid unhooked the engagement ring from the band. "I suspect we've got the rings part of this production taken care of."

My heart thumped as he slid the engagement ring onto my left ring finger. "Oh, honey, it's perfect."

Sid leaned over and kissed me so tenderly. I blinked back tears.

"Nick is looking rather disgustedly at us." I said taking the two bands and the promise ring and putting them in the ring box that had been in my purse.

Sid sighed. "Okay. I'm not trying to mess with his brain, but he is going to have to get used to the fact that we are more than just a couple now. I refuse to let him come between us."

"No." I winced at the twinge of guilt I felt, nonetheless. "That would not be right. And besides, kids are supposed to feel more secure when their parents are happy."

It was Sid's turn to wince. Then he looked at my purse.

"Why do you have a piece of strapping tape on that handle?" he asked. He had apparently not taken out his contacts before we'd boarded, which was another change for him.

I flushed slightly. "I started my period today. I want to be sure I get the tape on the mirror."

"Why? It's not like I'm going to get you pregnant." In addition to avoiding the whole bodily fluids thing, Sid was fixed, something he'd done shortly after Nick's conception.

"No. It's my breast self-exam." I'd already told him that the tape went on the mirror on the first day of my period and he'd darned well better not take it off. "The best time to do it is right after my period has ended. Only I used to forget a lot, so I figured out that if I put a reminder out on the first day of my period, I'm more likely to remember to do the exam when I'm done."

"Wouldn't a calendar work?"

"I already tried that. The problem is, I'm already dressed by the time I look at my calendar and it doesn't make sense to get undressed, if you know what I mean."

Sid nodded and shifted. It wasn't like he tracked my periods or anything. Why would he? But there had been enough issues with them early on that I'd gotten past being embarrassed about talking to him about it. If he'd shifted, I suddenly realized, it was because we were at that level of intimacy where it made sense to talk about it as part of our everyday lives.

It was and it wasn't weird. When it came to emotional intimacy, Sid and I had that down. In some ways, it almost felt like we were an old married couple finishing each other's sentences. But the rest of it, what with Nick and all, it felt like it was happening at light speed and neither Sid nor I was ready for it.

[Actually, when I shifted, I was wondering how we were going to work around your period in terms of our current activities. Though your point about everything changing so fast, that was very much the case. - SEH]

When we got home, there was more spoiled food in the refrigerator than not. I was annoyed, as was Sid, but it was the reality of our lives.

We got called out of town at odd intervals and that meant whatever groceries we had would either wait or go the way of all flesh.

"What are we going to do about dinner?" I asked Sid.

He shrugged. "What do you want?"

I yawned, the previous week and a half suddenly jumping on me.

"Ergh," I muttered. "Any way you can make dinner out of what we have?"

Sid smiled. "I should be able to."

As it turned out, Nick was already asleep in his room. Sid made up a stir-fry from the few vegetables that hadn't gone bad but would if we didn't do something with them. Nick still being out, we piled plenty of dried pepper flakes into the mix. The result was quite enjoyable. Even better was the time Sid and I were able to spend, well, making each other happy.

As we cuddled afterward, I nuzzled Sid.

"Maybe you should go sleep in with Nick," I muttered.

"No. I'm here with you. He's going to have to get used to it."

"I don't want to traumatize him."

"I agree, Lisapet. But I suspect it's going to traumatize him more if we aren't together. Okay?"

"Okay." I was pretty sleepy at that point. "I love you, Sid."

"I love you, Lisa. Goodnight."

"Goodnight, my sweet."

August 15 – 18, 1985

Dr. Robert Heilland is a trauma specialist who deals with FBI agents and other operatives. Sid and I had started seeing him the previous spring after I'd been kidnapped. The kidnapping had been traumatizing for both of us, but as it turned out, we each had plenty of other traumas to deal with, too. Sid had fought in the Vietnam war, which was hard enough, but had been pulled into intelligence work in boot camp and never released from it after he got back home. I had (okay, still have) a phobia of dead bodies, which sounds really strange, given my business, but it was the business that had done it to me. We both suffer from occasional nightmares about the first time we each killed someone.

The therapy was helping a lot, and we were only seeing Dr. Heilland every other week at that point. He's on the tallish side, with light gray hair, almost completely gone on top, and a neatly trimmed beard, basically, the comfortable uncle. He'd suggested that we bring Nick to that morning's session, so we did. Dr. Heilland explained that he didn't really work with children, but thought it would be helpful for Nick, not to mention help Dr. Heilland get some perspective on what Sid and I were dealing with.

He talked with Nick for about 20 minutes, then brought the boy out to the outer office.

"Okay, Sid, Lisa, come on in. Nick, will you please stay out here?"

"Sure," said Nick.

Sid looked at him. "In this room. If you have to use the bathroom, you knock on the door."

"Yes, sir." Nick sighed.

Dr. Heilland chuckled as he shut the door. "That was pretty specific."

I glanced over at Sid, then sat down on the couch next to him.

"We have to be with Nick," Sid said.

"He doesn't mean to get into trouble," I explained. "It's just that if there's a loophole, he'll find it and exploit it." I looked up at Dr. Heilland, suddenly insecure. "That is the right thing to do, isn't it?"

"Yes." Dr. Heilland laughed. "You two obviously know your kid and how to effectively deal with him."

"That's good to know." Sid squeezed my hand. "It's just going to be a really big adjustment. Oh, and Lisa and I are getting married."

"Really?" Dr. Heilland's eyebrows rose. "Lisa, how are you doing with that?"

"It was my idea." I took a deep breath and remembered why. "It's about sacrament. It's important to me and I think Sid and I deserve that."

"And you, Sid?"

"Well, I'm not doing it just to make her happy. That wouldn't work. But it's important to her and I'm happy to support that. It doesn't really make much difference to me beyond that. I've made my promise. She's made hers. That's the important part."

Dr. Heilland went on to ask us about how we felt about being full-time parents so suddenly, and we reminded him that we'd been expecting to take custody at some point. If it hadn't been for Rachel hiding her illness, we might even had have done it sooner. There was no question we loved the boy.

"I suppose the option exists that I could abandon him," Sid said finally. "But it's not an option I could live with. And we have been parents for a while now. Just not full-time." He frowned and shook his head. "Everything feels like we're making it up on the fly."

"You are," Dr. Heilland said. "But so does every other parent. Kids don't come with instruction manuals because each kid is different. What you've got going in your favor is that you two really understand Nick and based on what I heard from him and you, you three have a good relationship with each other. There's ninety percent of your battle. You've still got his grief to deal with, and with the other changes in your lives, it's going complicate things. But kids are resilient, especially when they are well-loved."

Sid nodded. "I just wish I didn't feel so lost."

Dr. Heilland laughed. "That's how you know you're a parent, Sid."

From Dr. Heilland's, we went to an early lunch because the movers from Sunnyvale were due at the condo. We still had to find time to buy groceries to replace all the food that had spoiled while we were gone.

"Why doesn't Conchetta come and cook?" Nick asked as Sid and I debated when best to go shopping.

"She only comes in two days a week while we're in the condo," Sid said. "There's not that much for her to do."

After lunch, I had Sid drop me off at the FBI building in Westwood. I went up to Henry James' office, chit-chatted with Angelique, his secretary, for a few minutes, then went in to see Henry and told him about the day before.

"Mittman didn't say why he wanted to know what was going on?" Henry asked.

"No, and he evaded my question when I asked."

"Hm." Henry looked at me. "You and Sid will be the ones looking into it. The Dragon is insisting that anything connected to O'Connor go to you two."

The Dragon was the head of Quickline.

I grimaced. "Not good timing."

"I know. But when is it ever? It's those Thirty-Four-As. They're easily spooked, for obvious reasons. Anyway, I hope you're up on the works of Kurt Vonnegut."

"Cat's Cradle," I said. "And Player Piano. Those are both Vonnegut titles."

Henry nodded. "That's how you know it's Thirty-Four-A."

"Okay. Well, I'd better get back. Oh, and I need a new handgun. SFPD took mine yesterday, and I don't want to wait until they release it."

Henry sighed and got up. "Come on. I'll give you a ride to the condo."

It was just the excuse. Henry had the equipment and paperwork in his car. I also picked up a transmitter for Nick.

"It's so we can keep tabs on him," I explained.

Henry wasn't convinced.

When I got back to the condo, all was chaos. The movers had arrived with the furniture and other things from Nick's old bedroom in Sunnyvale. Movers from the charity we'd called that morning waited to take whatever Nick didn't want. Then Sid and Nick had to follow the movers from Sunnyvale so that they could put whatever wouldn't fit in the condo into our storage unit. Then Nick's bedroom had to be re-arranged three or four times as Nick decided where he wanted things. We ended up going out to dinner that night since we still hadn't found time to get groceries and finally went to get them after dinner.

After lunch on Friday, Sid got called out on a pickup. Fortunately, Frank Lonnergan showed up and kept Nick busy with a guitar lesson. Nick is not the musician his father is. Frank is a professional musician but was having a very hard time making a living at it. In fact, the reason he lived at Esther's duplex was that she was supporting him. She's an engineer at one of the defense plants in El Segundo.

By the time Sid got back, Nick had mastered the riff from "Everybody Wants to Rule the World," so we sent him and Frank to watch

TV at Kathy and Jesse's place since we didn't have a TV in our condo, and they had a TV in their guest room.

Sid pulled out the microdot reader, which basically looks like one of those thinga-ma-jigs you use to look at your slides without putting them on a screen, only the magnification is considerably higher.

"It's the police report on Wednesday's incident," Sid said in wonder.

"Already. That was fast."

"No kidding. Not much here we don't already know, except who was in that van you apparently clipped."

"I did?"

"You blew out at least one of the tires." Sid smiled at me proudly. "Anyway, there were three guys, all Palestinian nationals, who got off thanks to diplomatic immunity."

"Palestinians?" I all but grabbed the microdot reader. "That doesn't make any sense. The cops don't know who the Palestinians were aiming at, either."

Sid closed his eyes. "We're looking for a stash of stolen U.S . weapons, right?"

"Yeah." Something triggered in my brain. "Sid, are you thinking that this could be one of those we'll sell weapons to the Middle East to fund someone in South America that we like kinds of things?"

"I have no idea."

It was one of those things that happened that wasn't common knowledge. [And I remember laughing our asses off when it did break. - SEH] Still, there wasn't much more we could do about it. At least, we didn't have to go out of town. We had enough to do to get Nick settled.

Esther showed up after work, and she and Frank joined Kathy, Jesse, Sid, Nick, and me for dinner that night in Kathy and Jesse's condo. Sid did the cooking at our place, but there wasn't room for everyone to eat there, so we brought it all over to Kathy and Jesse's.

Saturday, Sid somehow convinced Nick to go to the Huntington Library near Pasadena, and Mae and Neil joined us with the kids, which presented some problems in terms of active kids running around and priceless art treasures, but the kids behaved when they needed to, and it was a rousing success. Sid treated us all to dinner at a local seafood restaurant, and Mae even thanked him with a big old kiss on the cheek.

I was surprised Sunday morning when Nick said he'd go to mass with me. Nick's grandmother had been raising him in the Church until she passed. Rachel had left the Church and so the only time Nick went to mass was when I brought him. I had agreed with Sid that going to church should be Nick's choice, but I must admit, it felt pretty good that he'd chosen to go. We drove the Beemer because I was scheduled to bring Holy Communion to several shut-ins after mass. I was also serving as Eucharistic Minister that mass, so I left Nick with my purse in the pew out front with Jesse. Kathy was already in the sacristy. She was lectoring, namely reading one of the three readings for that mass. In fact, it was from Ephesians, and it was one of those weird bits of happenstance that Sid calls coincidence and I say it's why I believe.

Anyway, as I went into the sacristy, Maryann Dreyer was there. She was thin, perfectly tanned, with blond hair that had been teased out and glued into place. She and her husband, Michael, were the couple almost every parish has at least one of, on every committee, usually trying to throw their weight around. They had two daughters, I think the eldest was due to start college that year, and a son about Nick's age. Michael Dreyer was a real estate developer and often made a point of not so subtly reminding everybody what a big donor he was to the church. They were also the moralists I most dreaded.

"What are you doing here?" Maryann glared at me.

I wondered, at first, why she was there, then realized the ministers from the previous mass were still cleaning up the vessels. The Dreyers usually went and/or served at the nine o'clock mass, which had the traditional music and (horrible) choir.

"I'm scheduled to serve," I said, puzzled.

"I told them to take you off the schedule. We can't cause a scandal."

Kathy came over. "What are you talking about?"

"She's still living with that man." Maryann's face got even more pinched than usual. "And now they're supposedly getting married. You can't tell me that's living like brother and sister. She shouldn't be serving. It will cause scandal."

"What?" I gaped.

"You don't know what's going on!" Kathy snapped. "For all you know, she's staying with Jesse and me."

"Or maybe we're already married," I said.

"I do not care what you say." Maryann sniffed. "If you serve today, I am going to the archdiocese."

I swallowed. "Alright. Fine." My pix, a container for holding the blessed communion hosts, dangled from a chain around my neck and I fingered it. The last thing I wanted was to get Father John in trouble. "I won't. But I am going to communion."

Maryann flounced off.

"Lisa, you can't let her tell you what to do." Kathy glared after her.

"It's alright," I said, even though it wasn't. "I'll still bring the Sacrament to my shut-ins."

"Give me your pix, then. I'll get your hosts for you."

I pulled the chain from my neck and gave it to Kathy. I went out to the pew and sat down next to Nick, then nodded at Jesse.

"You'd better get back there," I said, blinking back my tears. "They'll be short a Eucharistic minister if you don't."

Jesse looked at me funny but went back to the sacristy.

"You okay, Lisa?" Nick's brow creased in worry.

"No, actually. I'm not. Something ugly just happened and it hurt." I took a deep breath. "But I am going to be the better person and rise above it." I pressed my fingers to my tear ducts. "Okay."

Truth be told, it was anything but okay. I'd seen certain members of the church change communion lines when they saw where I was serving. It couldn't be helped. I knew I was blameless. I shivered as the memory of the night before with Sid filled me with warmth and excitement. I knew Maryann would call it sin yet being with Sid that way felt like anything but. It was good and filled with joy and deep love. Afterward, when Sid kissed me goodnight, I almost cried, I loved him so much.

That mass was awkward hardly describes it. There was an undercurrent of tension that even the joyful music of the Guitar Choir couldn't break. The choir was led by Frank Lonnergan, and Esther was probably in the choir loft with him. I wondered if those two would be Maryann's next target. At least, Esther's cousin lived with them.

Father John's eyes had a grim cast to them as he began the mass. Kathy did the second reading, which said to get rid of all bitterness, passion, and anger, and to be kind and to follow the way of love. It almost looked as though she wanted to knock Maryann over the head with the lectionary, or readings book. John's face was not any happier as he read the gospel for the day. When he'd finished, he pulled out the sheet of paper with his sermon notes, as he usually did while everyone was sitting down after standing for the gospel. Then he crumpled the sheet into a tight ball. Kathy gasped - she had returned to the pew after reading. My jaw almost fell open. John was really angry. I don't think any of us had ever seen that before. Annoyed, occasionally cranky, yes, we'd seen that. But furious? Never.

"This morning," he said into the microphone at the ambo. "Something mean and ugly happened. A parishioner, filled with bitterness, passion, and anger, behaved in a manner that was unbelievably not loving toward another of our parishioners. Now, who these people are, I do not want to get into. The specifics of the dispute are not important, either. What happened is. This person judged someone else in a way that was hurtful and false. There is no place for that kind of behavior in a Christian church. Absolutely no place. Now, we are frail beings. We judge others all the time. So, let's be clear on what judgmentalism is. It is deciding that you know the state of someone else's soul better than that someone else. Now, we may think we are being kind and even caring. Or maybe that's our excuse. Either way, there is a world of difference between reaching out in love to a brother or sister struggling with some sin and judging them. How do we know? If your concern is not about a specific behavior, but about who that person is, you are judging them. If you assume the worst in a person's behavior or attitude, especially without knowing all the facts, then you are judging. If you get mad that this person is not listening to you, then you are judging this person and this person is probably not going to listen to you." He paused as his eyes swept over the congregation. "That's all I have to say today. We believe in one God..."

I don't think there was anybody in that church that morning who wasn't shell-shocked. We scrambled to our feet to finish reciting the Creed and mass went on. I did change lines to go to communion, but that was because I wanted John to see me. He nodded as he placed the host in my hand. After communion, while the other Eucharistic ministers and John were clearing up, Kathy returned to the altar and waited with the other ministers who would be delivering the Eucharist to the sick and shut in. John glanced over at me, then filled the pix. Kathy made the announcements, then came back to the pew. Nick and I squeezed back so that she could sit next to Jesse before we all stood for the recessional. As the notes of the final hymn drifted away, I picked up my purse.

"Kathy, can I have my pix?" I asked.

"It's in your purse," she said.

I looked and it was. "Wow. I didn't see you do that." It was as smooth a drop as I'd ever seen. "That's pretty impressive."

"Think so?" Kathy smiled and Jesse squeezed her shoulder. "John wants to see you in the sacristy."

My gut clenched. "Goody. Nick, why don't you wait out by the car? I'll be right there."

John was hanging up his vestments as I went in. He nodded me back toward his vesting area. The ten-thirty mass ministers were finishing cleaning vessels and saying hi to the noon mass ministers who were coming in. Noon was one of the two Spanish masses in the parish, so the chatter was largely in Spanish.

John looked at me. "Do you feel you are in a state of sin?"

"No," I said softly. "I went to communion." Going to communion when you're in a state of mortal sin is a massive no-no.

"I didn't think so." John sighed then spoke in measured tones. "Do not give in to Maryann Dreyer or anybody like that ever again."

"But she was going to go to the archdiocese."

He loomed over me. "It's my job to worry about that. Not yours. Do not do it again."

I quailed. He's a really big man. "Yes, John."

"I mean it. We can't let the Dreyers of this world win or it will tear our church apart. Do you understand me?"

"Yes, John."

He backed away a little. "Are you feeling guilty about anything?"

"Not really. I mean, you did say not condemned."

"Lisa, I do not give a damn what you and Sid do. It's none of my business unless you're feeling guilty about it. And it's nobody else's business, period. You two love each other and are committed to each other. That's all I need to worry about." He sighed. "And by the way, I personally told Lety Sandoval to keep you on the Eucharistic Minister schedule, and she's perfectly happy to." He smiled weakly. "In fact, she asked if she could drop Maryann. Now, get out of here. You've got shut-ins to visit."

Nick was waiting right by the car, and I thanked him for it.

"Was that sermon about what got you upset before mass?" he asked after we got in. He ran the window down to let out some of the hot air and put the air conditioning on high.

"I'm afraid it was, Nick." I started the engine and slowly backed out and around all the cars coming into the church parking lot. "There are just a lot of people who don't understand your father and me, and some of them think we shouldn't even like each other, let alone love each other."

"I hope Dad doesn't get too mad when he hears about this."

I stared straight ahead at the road. "Yeah. Talk about another conversation I do not want to have."

Fortunately, my shut-ins weren't worried about my relationship with Sid. Mrs. Salcido saw the engagement ring on my hand and squealed with joy.

"I have prayed for this!" she cried, holding my left hand. "Gracías a nos Madre!"

"You may hear that he's not exactly a saint," I said, smiling.

"You will make him one, mija. I am so happy for you." Then she reached out and pulled Nick next to her wheelchair. "And this is his beautiful boy. Are you happy for your mama?"

Nick giggled. "Yeah."

The mood back at the condo was not good. Frank and Esther had followed Kathy and Jesse there. They were all four furious. As for Sid, he was pacing, and it was a good thing that the Dreyers were not within reach of his fists. He looked up as I opened the door.

"Oh, honey!" He pulled me into his arms.

"I'm fine, Sid. Father John and I talked it out. It's over and done with."

Sid let me go. "I am seriously considering filing suit."

I rolled my eyes and flopped onto the couch. "I doubt we have damages." I looked over at Frank and Esther. "You guys gonna be okay?"

Nick flopped down next to me, and I cuddled him.

"If she comes after us, she comes after us. I don't care," Esther said then looked at Sid. "Besides, she don't hate Frank the way she hates you."

"What is that all about?" Kathy asked, sitting down on the couch next to me.

"Oh, she had it in for Sid even before she met him," I said. "But then there was that teen dance a couple years ago that Sid helped chaperon."

"Yeah." Esther laughed as Sid groaned. "That was that time you had Frank play 'I Get Around,' and you two danced. That was cute."

"Except Maryann pinned me down at the punch bowl," I continued. "She was all up in arms because a youth group leader was living with a man. Then Sid came up and I just introduced him by name, and she went on about living with a man, and Sid said why not? Sharing a house like brother and sister, what could be wrong with that? Maryann had to back off a little. But then those four girls that were doing that Hey, Guy thing?"

Jesse choked. "I remember them. Brittany somebody."

"Our Brittany?" Kathy asked.

"Not the current one," I said. There had been a lot of Brittanys among the teens. "It was some other kid, and I don't remember the rest of their names. They're all gone, anyway. But you know, they'd stalk a boy or a man, then screech 'Hey, guy, wanna get lucke-e-e-e?'"

"Oh, them." Kathy shook her head and shivered. "We couldn't get them to stop for love nor money."

"Sid found a way." I looked fondly at him.

"What? I opened my wallet and asked how much?" Sid shrugged.

"Right in front of Maryann Dreyer." I couldn't help laughing.

Frank hooted. "Oh, I would have loved to have seen her face."

"They never did it again," Sid said.

"It gets worse." I shook my head.

Sid rolled his eyes. "I was trying to guarantee that I would never be asked to chaperon a teen dance again." He looked at Nick. "That still stands, by the way."

I sighed. "After I pointed out to Maryann that Sid was bluffing because he wouldn't touch an underage girl, she thought it was such a funny joke. Until Sid made a pass at her, which she put off to joking. Then when she asked how he knew me, he told her I was his housemate."

Esther laughed. "I can see why she hates you two. But she's still a narrow-minded witch."

Okay, witch was not the word Esther used.

"There's not much we can do about her," I said then glared at Sid. "And I do not want to sue them. It will just give them more power because we'll be persecuting them."

Later, Sid held me as we lay together in bed.

"You're not feeling guilty, are you?"

"No." I looked at him. I really wasn't.

"Then why didn't you stand up to Dreyer? You usually do."

"I didn't want to get John in trouble."

"Hm." He didn't sound convinced. "Just remember, my darling, moralists and social norms? Our job is to buck them."

"Or work with them. That's why you wear clothes."

Sid may be a clotheshorse, but he's perfectly comfortable with being in the raw. He chuckled and kissed me one more time and we went to sleep.

August 19, 1985

As Sid and I had told Dr. Heilland, we had been anticipating taking custody of Nick. In fact, one of the things Sid had done the previous winter was check out various schools in the area and he'd concluded that my church's school was pretty darned good, and because I was active at the parish, that just made it easier.

When we told Nick that Monday that we had an appointment that morning to register him at the school, Nick got upset. I think it hit him that he was not going back to Sunnyvale. He cried and we held him, but we also held firm. One thing that perked him up was when we arrived at the principal's office and Sister Maria Campos not only knew me but greeted me as a friend. We'd worked on some committee or another. Maria passed Nick onto one of the teachers so that Nick could take his placement tests, then ushered Sid and me into the office.

"Lisa, naughty, naughty. Where have you been hiding that cutie?" Maria grinned as she arranged some paperwork on her chronically messy desk.

Maria was a touch on the filled-out side, with dark hair and a round face. Her brown eyes generally sparkled with, if not mischief, at least something close. The kids at the school mostly loved her. The parents were mostly relieved.

"I hid him with his mother," I replied.

Maria's eyebrows rose. "Good to see you, Sid."

Sid nodded and shifted. "Good to see you, Maria."

I wasn't sure if it was the fact that Maria didn't wear a habit or simply the fact that she was a nun, but Sid was still really uncomfortable around her, never mind how friendly he'd gotten with Father John. [It was all the nonsense I'd heard about nuns for years. I knew it was bullshit, even before I got to know Maria. Why those ridiculous stereotypes stuck with me, I have no idea. But it took getting to know Maria to banish them. – SEH]

"Anyway, Nick's mother passed away earlier this month," I said. "We've been wanting to take custody, so we're okay."

"Oh, that's too bad. I hear you guys are getting married. Was that before or after the mom passed?"

"Before," said Sid shortly.

"Oh. Nice." She paused and smiled. "Here's the new parent drill. When you enroll Nick here, you are agreeing to forty hours a year in school volunteer work." Maria rolled her eyes. "Sorry, Lisa, the other things you do in the parish don't count. It has to be for the school."

Sid grunted in disgust.

"I know, Sid." Maria sighed. "It's not fair. The hours Lisa puts in. But if we didn't require parents to volunteer nothing would get done around here."

"I can imagine," Sid said.

I winced. "Alright. What needs doing?"

Maria looked at Sid thoughtfully. "I think something that requires minimal contact with the other parents. Somehow, Sid, I think you might be happier that way."

Sid's eyebrows rose. "I might be."

"You guys are writers, right? How about taking on the parents newsletter?"

Sid looked like he was about to retch.

"We'll take it," I said. The last thing I wanted was Sid on a committee with people who were at least as judgmental and controlling as the Dreyers, even if they were a lot more progressive.

Sid can't technically read my mind, but I think he got my concern. "Sounds like we can make it work."

"Alright. Terrific. You've filled out all your forms." She flipped through several sheets of paper. "Here's your packet covering tuition, uniforms and where to get them, grade reports, the behavior code." She grinned. "I'm guessing Nick can be a bit of a handful."

"He's really good at finding loopholes," I said, almost helplessly. "But he doesn't mean to get into trouble."

Maria laughed. "My kind of kid." She scratched her chin thoughtfully. "I think Nick and I are going to have an extended conversation when he's done with his tests." She smiled at Sid. "Look. I get it, Sid. You're not comfortable with the religion thing or the parenting thing."

"We've been his parents for at least eighteen months," Sid growled.

"Not full-time," Maria said, grinning even more wildly. "That's different and I think you guys know that already." Her face softened. "You guys are going to be okay. It's going to be a little bumpy, but you'll be fine. It's all about love. You love Nick. I can see that. He's very lovable, too."

Sid finally relaxed. "He is. I'm glad you see it."

"Great." Maria stood. "Nick has work to do, and I'll bet you two do, as well." She paused. "You know, I am really glad he's here. It will give me more of a chance to hang with Lisa."

I flushed a little. "Thanks, Maria."

Sid and I got up and left the office. Once outside, in the parking lot, Sid sighed.

"Would you mind terribly if I took a walk by myself?" he asked.

"Not at all," I said.

Sid took a deep breath and let it out. "Thanks."

I wandered over to the rectory. John was in his office and looked up happily when he saw me at his door.

"How are you doing?" he asked.

I shrugged. "Getting along. It's been a bit of a morning. We're getting Nick registered at the school."

"Ah. How's it going?"

"Nick was a little upset, at first. Not the school. Just being someplace else."

"That makes sense. And Sid?"

I winced. "I think he's feeling like he's bitten off more than he can chew. Finding out about the volunteer requirement after yesterday was a little hard on him."

John frowned. "He did not react well to yesterday, did he?"

"He was talking lawsuit."

John laughed deeply. "Now that I would support."

"Please don't, John! I really do not want that to happen. It would only make things worse."

John made a face. "You're probably right." He looked at me. "How are you and Sid otherwise?"

"Very good. Why?"

"Change. You're planning your marriage, which I'm willing to bet was not in Sid's life plan."

"It wasn't in mine, either."

John acknowledged that with a shrug. "You're also now full-time parents to an almost adolescent. It's a lot to take on."

"It's what we've got. We have a solid commitment to each other."

"That I do know." He smiled and sat up. "Oh, before I forget. We've got the liturgical ministers retreat in September. Tess Forsythe says she could use some help."

"Okay." I sighed. "Does she mind me being a fallen woman?"

John laughed again. "Tess? I wouldn't worry about it. She may even be in the church right now. Why don't you go see?"

Tess Forsythe was a widow in her early seventies. She was tall and willowy and absolutely not the woman you would ever want to cross.

She was on the altar clearing away dead flowers from the offerings in front.

"Lisa!" She grinned when she saw me. "Is it true? He's going to marry you?"

I rolled my eyes. "Well, we have agreed to marry."

Tess laughed. "Better to do it that way, kiddo. So, what brings you here?"

"Father John sent me. He said you needed help with the liturgical ministers retreat."

"What I need are speakers. Can you do a talk on servanthood?"

"Sure. If I'm not called out of town."

Tess rolled her eyes. "I understand, but what a pain in the butt."

Suddenly, the haunting notes of the old Phantom of the Opera theme burst through the organ pipes on the wall. Okay, it was actually Bach's Toccata and Fugue in D Minor. Down the aisle, Juanita Llanez jumped and let out a startled "*Santa Maria*!" and crossed herself. As the music continued, some other woman began crying down near the vestibule and Juanita ran down that way, presumably explaining in fast Spanish. I looked up at the choir loft in the back. I couldn't see who was playing the organ, but I had a bad feeling I knew. Tess actually giggled.

"Sid?" I asked her.

She nodded. "He's been doing it since last winter. John told him he could practice on the organ if he liked. He always starts with Phantom of the Opera, scares the snot out of us, plays a few more tunes, then comes down and flirts with all the old ladies to apologize." Tess even giggled again. "We love him. It's our weekly thrill."

I smiled despite myself. "Far be it from me to disrupt that." I glanced up at the choir loft, suddenly aware that Sid had been out part of most Monday mornings since the winter before. I checked my watch. "However, his son should be done with his placement tests at the school in about another forty-five minutes."

"Son?"

"Yeah. We had to take custody earlier this month. His mother passed."

"I'm so sorry." Tess looked mildly surprised. "I didn't know Sid was married before."

"Um. He wasn't."

Tess flat out laughed. "And the kid?"

"At least as charming and adorable as his father," I said. "Can you do me a favor, please? In between the flirting, can you let Daddy know that I'll take care of fetching his son?"

"Happy to." The gleam in Tess' eyes almost worried me.

I took a walk and got back to the school just in time. Nick came out of the first-grade room looking washed out.

"You okay, sweetie?" I asked.

He sighed. "I guess."

Maria emerged from her office. "Well, how did you do, young man?"

"I dunno." Nick looked up at her, vaguely afraid.

"It's okay, Nick," Maria said. "Why don't you and I have a little chat?"

"Really?"

"Oh, come on. Like you haven't seen the inside of a principal's office before?"

Nick groaned. "I don't try to get into trouble. I just do."

"Not an uncommon affliction at all." Maria patted him on the shoulder. "Come on. Let's see if we can find some ways to avoid problems."

Nick looked at me for help, then realized that Maria was a friend of mine. I believe he thought that could work in his favor. Maybe it would, maybe it wouldn't. He knew he couldn't get away with a lot with me. And I knew Maria wouldn't be any easier on him. Still, she seemed to have the right touch with Nick and that meant a lot to me.

Sid showed up about fifteen minutes later.

"Nick?" he asked.

"Chatting with Maria." I grinned at him. "I hope you haven't shorted the old ladies on their weekly thrill."

Shocked, Sid looked at me, then laughed. "No. I have been appropriately shameless." He paused. "You're not feeling jealous, are you?"

"Not really. You're not going to act on it, so who cares? They get a little titillation, you prove you still have it. I'm happy."

He smiled, then put his arm around my shoulders. "How did I end up in this place?"

"As I understand it, the condom broke."

Sid laughed. "Yeah. Right."

A couple minutes later, Nick came bounding out of the office.

"Dad!" he yelped, then headed out the door.

"I'll go after him," Sid said and followed.

Maria appeared in the doorway, still smiling. "Oh, he is going to be fun to have around here."

"What do you mean?" I asked.

"High energy, very bright, very curious." Maria looked after him. "Has he ever been on Ritalin? For the hyper-activity?"

I thought. "I don't think so. I'm pretty sure he hasn't been on anything since we've known him, but his medical records aren't the most complete. He changed pediatricians when he was ten, and because his mom was a doctor, his new doctor didn't see him all that much."

"A couple other things." Maria's face grew serious. "We were talking about you guys taking custody of him, and he explained about how his mother made him keep her cancer a secret. He was a little angry that you guys took so long to make up your minds about it. So, I asked why it took so long, and he clammed up suddenly. Just said that you had a good reason."

"Oh. I think I know what that's about." I shrugged. "It's no big deal."

Only just our second, secret, life.

"Also, he seems a little worried that you, specifically, are not as excited about having him."

"Oh, no!"

Maria patted my arm. "He knows you love him, and he loves you. My guess is that he's trying to figure out where he fits into your lives, and with you and Sid being newly engaged, it puts a whole new dynamic on whatever relationship you had before. Just don't be surprised if you get some acting out. Between his grief and his age, it's perfectly normal. In fact, I'd probably be worried if he doesn't."

Lety Sandoval came hurrying into the office at that moment. She's somewhat on the short side with dark hair, has a comfortable figure, and is usually in motion. In addition to coordinating the Eucharistic Minister schedule, she works on the parish festival committee, supervises community sports leagues for two of her three boys, and is probably on two or three other committees. I tried to remember which school committee she ran.

"Oh, hi, Lisa." She smiled warmly at me. "What brings you over to this side of the parish?"

"We took custody of Sid's son. We just got him registered here."

"In fact," Maria said. "Nick will be in Josh's class."

Lety's eyes lit up and she looked at me. "That's great. Josh is my oldest. Hey, I have an idea. I'm taking Josh and a few of his friends to the mall tomorrow afternoon. Why don't we bring your kid along? He'll get a chance to make some friends. I mean, really, new schools are the pits, and this way he'll know some of the kids before school starts."

"That's so nice of you, Lety. Thanks." I thought it over briefly. "I'll double check with Sid, but if Nick wants to go, I don't see why not. He just may not want to go. His mother passed away earlier this month and he's been a little clingy."

"Oh, poor baby. Well, give me a call tonight and let me know." She turned to Maria. "About the school's festival table?"

I left the office and found Sid and Nick standing in the shade of the school building. Sid's forehead was beaded with sweat, and the arm pits of Nick's shirt were drenched. We went home and Sid made lunch. Unfortunately, neither Jesse nor Kathy were home, so Nick had to stay in the condo with us, which was pretty hard on him. After we ate lunch, Nick went to his room.

I quietly told Sid about Lety Sandoval's invitation.

"That might be a very good thing," Sid said. "Let's go ask him if he wants to go."

Nick decided he wanted to go, so Sid and I went back to our writing work. Or I did after I called Lety. I had mail to open and a rough draft to write. Sid was doing interviews for a real estate piece he was working on. A few minutes later, I had to get up and go over to the part of the dining table where my sewing stuff was, and Nick was playing with Motley.

"Nick, can you please not play around my sewing stuff?" I said softly because Sid was on the phone with a headset on and typing away on his computer.

"Okay."

I went back to my desk. One of the puzzles Sid and I were trying to work out was how to set up our office - or offices - at the house. We'd each had our own office when I first came to work for Sid. But we were a little stuck on whether to keep individual rooms or just one big one. We both agreed that it was very pleasant being able to look across our desks at each other and to not have to go back and forth between rooms all the time. The problem was if one of us had to do a phone interview while the other was trying to get something written or edited. Or if we both had phone interviews at the same time.

Sid had Long John in his lap and the kittens were draped over the living room and dining area. Nick began playing with Motley again. I went back to trying to concentrate on the mail. A minute later, there was a crash over by the dining area. A plastic box of straight pins had gone flying and was upended on the carpet. Sid looked over and I waved him back to his interview as I got up to deal with it.

"Nick, I asked you not to play over here," I said, my voice getting tight. "This is why. Now, you need get these picked up right away."

"Sorry."

"Get the magnet. You need to get every one of these pins up. Straight pins in carpet hurt, and we don't want Motley or one of the cats to get stuck, do we?"

"No!"

I went back to my desk. Sid ended his call and took the headset off.

"Everything okay?" he asked.

"It's fine. Did we decide to put wood floors in the workroom?"

"I think so. I'll make a note for the architect just in case." Sid shuffled through the papers on his desk, then cursed. "I forgot to tell you. Your mother called yesterday while you were at church. She wanted to know if you'd made up your mind about the hotel for the reception."

I sighed. "I do have to get that figured out. What do you think?"

"Whatever you want, honey." He put his headset back on and dialed another number.

I glared at him briefly, then went back to trying to concentrate.

Sid made dinner for all five of us that night and we ate at Kathy and Jesse's. I went back to our condo to get some sewing done, but then remembered that I had to look at the hotel brochures and pick a place. I went to get the brochures out of my purse and found something else instead.

Back when we were moving out of the house, the sewing pattern had fallen out of one of the boxes and gotten kicked into a corner when the movers had come. I'd found it as Sid and I were getting ready to leave so that the builders could move in and I did what I usually did. I stuck it in my purse and forgot about it. The pattern was for a pretty dress of lace or chiffon with a high collar, softly puffed long sleeves, and a full skirt. The envelope featured a photo of the knee-length version in black on a blond model. But next to it was the floor-length version in white lace in a drawing showing it on a woman with her hair up and flowers in it. I put the pattern aside, then got out the brochures.

At nine, I was no closer to a decision. Sid and Nick came back to our condo. Nick ran ahead to his room and Sid followed. As soon as Sid emerged, I went into the bedroom and gave Nick a goodnight kiss.

"How are you feeling, sweetie?" I toyed with his dark, wavy hair, so much like his father's.

He was sleeping on the top bunk of his bunk bed, so his face was level with mine. I wasn't sure where he'd put his glasses.

"I like it here." He made a face. "But I'm still sad."

"That's okay." I smiled softly at him. "It's going to take time is all."

"That's what Dad says."

"Then it must be true. I love you, Nick. Goodnight."

"Goodnight, Lisa."

I kissed him again, then turned out the light as I left the room.

Sid stood over the table, looking at the brochures.

"What do you think?" I asked him.

He shrugged. "Whatever you want."

"What I want is help," I said crossly. "I don't want to make all these decisions by myself."

"What about your mother?"

"Okay. She has a say, too. I mean she is paying for it, and we're not going to get out of that one. She's been saving for too long. But I don't want to do this without you." I sighed. "I was kind of hoping you'd be more interested."

"I'm interested. You haven't really had that much to say about it except for when your mother was around, so I thought maybe you didn't want me to be that involved."

I flopped into one of the dining room chairs. "You and Mama can plan the whole darned thing if you want." I winced. "Okay, maybe not. I don't know. I wanted to keep it to fifty people, and we've got over a hundred already, and you know we're going to be adding to it. And Mama's right. We can't drop the relatives. I was thinking about canceling it after all and then I found this in my purse."

I reached over and handed him the sewing pattern. Sid shrugged.

"So?" he asked.

"I think I found my wedding dress."

He looked at the envelope again. "Black?"

"No." I laughed. "The drawing."

Sid frowned as he looked at the envelope again. "You know I'm not very good at visualizing these things." He looked at me, then back at the pattern. "But it does look like your style."

I took the pattern from him. "The funny thing is, I wasn't even thinking about the dress when I found this. I've been wanting to make it for a while, anyway. And it just seems right." I looked up at him. "Do you like it?"

"From what I see of it, I like it."

"That's good." I smiled softly down at the pattern. "I want to wear this dress. And I kind of want to have a wedding."

"Then that's what we'll do."

"Assuming we can find the right place for the reception." I sat up and looked dismally at the brochures.

Sid sat down next to me. "Any we can eliminate off the top?"

"Larger venues. I don't want any excuses to grow that guest list any bigger than a hundred and fifty."

"This place looks interesting."

"But the food wasn't that good."

We eventually got it settled and went to bed. Later, I woke up. Sid was quiet for a change - he talks in his sleep a lot. Soft crying came from the other room.

"Oh, no," I sighed, rocking the waterbed as I struggled up.

"Wha...?" Sid grunted. He lifted his head blinking.

"It's Nick. I think he's had a nightmare."

Sid groaned softly.

"I'll take care of it," I said.

I got a robe on, went to Nick's room, and opened the door.

"Nick, are you okay?"

"I was all alone again," he said, still weeping.

I climbed the ladder to his bunk, then sat down next to him with my feet hanging over the edge.

"It's alright," I said softly and rubbing his back. "You're not alone."

"Lisa, do you want me?"

"Of course, I do, Nick. I love you."

"Mom always said I should just get used to being alone."

"I'm not going to let that happen. No matter what, you are not going to be alone."

"But if you and Dad..."

"Yes, that's always possible. But I will make sure that there will be somebody to take care of you if your dad and I can't. We've got lots of people who love us, so you'll be taken care of, and you won't be alone."

He fell asleep a few minutes later. I softly kissed his forehead, then carefully got off the bunk.

Sid was still awake. "Well?"

"Nightmare. The one where he's the only person left on earth." I put the robe on its hook in the closet and got into bed.

Sid sighed.

"Sid. I want to ask Mae and Neil if they'll take care of Nick if anything happens to us."

"Good idea. I'll call Whiteman after you do. Get it in the wills pronto."

I nodded and snuggled up next to him. This was our life and how it was going to be.

August 20 – 21, 1985

We made sure Nick was out walking Motley with Jesse when Sid and I called Mae and Neil. They were perfectly happy to agree to taking Nick, then asked us if we'd do the same for their kids. All it took was one look between us and Sid and I agreed. Sid called his lawyer and asked him to amend our wills. Then he had to leave to do an interview in person and make a pickup.

Lety Sandoval arrived with Josh right after lunch. Lety introduced her son, a slight boy with dark coloring and wild black hair wearing a Dodgers t-shirt. Josh politely shook my hand, then Nick invited him to see his room.

"I can't thank you enough," I told Lety.

"I'm more than happy to." She paused. "I kind of don't want to say anything. It's just pettiness. But I don't want you blindsided if it catches up with you."

"If what catches up with me."

"Maryann Dreyer's boy, Jason. He's in Josh and Nick's class, too. He was going to come with us, then Maryann said he couldn't because she didn't want her son playing with that diseased boy."

"Who? Nick?"

"She's convinced Sid must have AIDS and given it to Nick. I know that's ridiculous, so don't worry."

My heart stopped. "Sid's been tested. It came back negative." I may have been overstating that, given that we were still waiting to test again.

Lety's eyes rose.

"Sid's straight," I said, feeling a little frantic. "He's just at risk because he used to sleep around a lot."

"I'd heard that." Lety shrugged. "Look, my husband, the orthopedic surgeon, has been keeping up on it, and Reuben says there's no way you can get it from casual contact, so I'm not the least bit worried about Nick. And you say Sid tested negative. Then we're fine." She sighed. "Actually, I'm kind of glad we don't have Jason with us. Josh really likes him, but Jason is mean a lot of times. I don't know what's going on with him, but he's pretty angry."

"That's too bad."

Sid arrived home at that moment and said hello to Lety, then Josh and Nick burst out of Nick's room. Nick had changed to his Giants t-shirt and the two boys were knee-deep in happy squabbling over the two teams. Josh politely shook Sid's hand. Sid gave Nick some money, then the two took off down the hall to the elevators.

Lety laughed as she headed out the door. "I'll bring him back right before dinner time."

"Thanks!" I called.

I shut the door and turned. "Okay, what happened with the pickup and how did your interview go?"

Sid was smiling at me lecherously. "Did she just say Nick won't be back until dinner time?"

"Sid." I shifted, the temptation growing. "We should talk about the pickup and there's work to do."

"I know. But all I want to do right now is get you naked and screaming."

I swallowed. "I don't scream."

"Oh, you most certainly do." His voice purred with anticipation.

"Well." I couldn't help smiling. "I suppose it would be nice to not be quite so inhibited."

Sid and I had been trying to keep the noise level down so we didn't wake and embarrass Nick.

"I'll go get a pair of jeans on." He headed for the bedroom.

I followed. "Can I watch you undress?"

He yipped in joy. "Yes! As long as I get to watch you undress."

Later, we snuggled, feeling quite content, indeed.

"What about that pickup?" I asked, not really feeling like talking about work, but knowing we had to.

"We'll have to leave tomorrow morning." Sid kissed my shoulder. "We've got to go track down Player Piano, who is, presumably, the only person who can make sense of that bit of paper that Cat's Cradle gave you."

"Terrific. What about Nick?"

"We'll have to take him with us. I'm not wild about it, but I don't want to leave him here."

"We'll have to leave him sometimes."

"But he's still so scared that we'll leave and he'll never see us again." He frowned. "It shouldn't be that difficult. There's a string of safe houses that we need to check out. Hopefully, Player Piano will be at one of them, we can make the delivery and go home and let Division Thirty-Four-Alpha worry about that arms stash."

"So, why did we get tagged with flushing out Player Piano?"

Sid sighed. "It's connected to Congressman O'Connor. In fact, he's the primary suspect in the weapons theft and murder of Cat's Cradle. His aide... What's his name?"

"Karl Mittman."

"He's been nosing around and pushing the Feds to find Player Piano, or whoever Cat's Cradle was trying to meet, or something like that."

"He knows that Cat's Cradle was meeting somebody? He didn't tell me that."

"I know. O'Connor gets some pretty interesting intelligence and not a lot of it gets to the other committee members. The other reasons we got tagged to find Player is that A- you still have that piece of paper, and B- thanks to Mittman, they want Special Agent Linda Devereaux to do the asking at the safe houses."

"Goody, goody, gum-drops."

"That's about the size of it." Sid shifted and looked around. "What time is it?"

I realized I still had my watch on. "Almost four."

"Guess we'd better get up and get dressed. We've got a lot to get done tonight." Sid sat up and scratched his chin. The dark stubble had already gotten rather thick, which is why Sid shaves twice a day. "I'll go ahead and get shaved, too."

It was a busy night. Lety and Josh brought Nick back around five-thirty. We had writing work to juggle, not to mention pets to arrange for. Thank God, Jesse and Kathy volunteered to take care of the animals. I couldn't believe how complicated it had all gotten. But it was how our life was. We'd told Kathy and Jesse that we'd been asked to so an extended story out of town and they seemed to believe it. I also had a couple errands to run, including a bookstore to purchase a certain paperback novel.

I asked Nick how the mall trip had gone when I went in to kiss him goodnight.

"We had a great time," Nick said. "I really like Josh."

"I'm glad," I said.

Sid followed me into the room, then kissed Nick, as well. Then we went back to packing and preparing.

"How did our lives get so complicated?" I asked Sid as we cuddled that night.

"You're asking me that?"

"Oh," I sighed. "You know those safe houses?"

"Yeah?"

"They're a chain of motels."

"I noticed that."

"I looked them up in Dunn and Bradstreet."

Since Sid and I did a lot of business articles, I'd talked him into buying the popular business reference, even though it had cost us a fortune. It still saved us a lot of errands to the UCLA library.

"And…?"

"One of the owners is Dale O'Connor."

"No kidding."

Okay. Sid did not use the word kidding.

"I don't see how that affects us," Sid continued.

"I don't, either." I played with the hair on his chest, my fingers finding their way to his nipples.

Sid let out a deeply satisfied grunt.

"I do want to get some sleep tonight," he said, nonetheless.

I pulled my hand away. "I'm sorry."

His hand caught mine. "It's fine, my love." He kissed my fingers. "But we do need to get some sleep."

Truth be told, I have no idea why he was worried about the sleep part of it. The first thing Sid does when he gets on a plane is take out his contacts and goes to sleep. I was still happy about getting some sleep that night. I do not sleep on planes as easily as he does and there was Nick to keep an eye on.

Sid, being the morning person he is, had found an early flight to St. Louis, so we were up earlier than normal. At least, we didn't have to go running. Sid showered first and I did my breast exam, since it was already time again. By the time I got out of the shower, Sid had shaved and was brushing his teeth. I got the toothpaste on my toothbrush and was about to put the tube in the toiletries bag when Sid pulled it out of my hand.

"I know this is trivial and petty, but it's been driving me nuts." He tightened the cap on the tube and began flattening the bottom. "I really hate it when you squeeze from the middle. I don't know why, but I do."

"Okay," I said through the foam.

"You don't mind?"

I shrugged. "Not really."

"Okay. Since you don't mind and I do, we can squeeze from the bottom."

I spat into the sink. "Sure."

He'd made the odd face or two in the mornings before, so I knew the tube squeezing was, in fact, getting to him. But I think the reason it did just then was the trip. Neither he nor I were that excited about bringing Nick with us. We had little idea what we were up against and did not like the idea of risking Nick's neck along with ours. Then there was also that Sid really doesn't like flying. He gets on planes all the time, so it's not like he's got a phobia about it. But it is why he tends to conk out as soon as the plane taxis toward the runway.

We made it to the airport in good time and let Nick run around in the hopes that he wouldn't get too antsy on the flight. Once we got on the plane, Nick made it clear that he wanted the window seat and that he wanted Sid to sit next to him. We were in the business class, too. Sid usually preferred first class, but we didn't want to attract attention by looking too prosperous. In fact, we were wearing vacation clothes instead of business wear. I again had my full wedding ring set on my left hand and Sid wore his wedding band. However, with only two seats on each side of the aisle, that meant I was across the aisle from Sid and Nick.

Sure enough, Sid was out like a light the second the plane left the gate. He stirred just long enough to put his seat back once he could and went back to muttering in his sleep. Fortunately, the noise of the plane drowned that out. I was a little surprised at how well I'd adapted to his nightly monologue.

"When are they going to start the movie?" Nick shouted over his father.

He was the only kid in the section, and I'd noticed an odd glare or two from the other businessmen there. I sighed and got out of my seat.

"Son, please keep your voice down." I leaned over the seats. "You'll wake your father."

"No, I won't."

I glared at him. "As for the movie, it will probably start after they've served lunch."

Nick flopped back into his seat, the disdain radiating off him.

"And watch your attitude, as well."

He rolled his eyes, but I pretended not to see it. Nick did have a point. It's not easy to wake Sid from a sound sleep. I went back to my seat and picked up my book. Every so often, I'd check on Nick. He did some reading, listened to his Walkman for a few minutes. Kept charming the bejeebers out of the flight attendants. He's his father's son, no question about it. I offered up a couple prayers that he wouldn't turn out to be as randy as his father had been. And in some ways, still was. I shifted as I thought about the night before.

Right after lunch was served, Nick appeared in the aisle next to my seat.

"I'm bored," he announced.

I checked my watch. "The movie should start soon."

He nodded at the empty window seat next to me. "Can I sit next to you?"

"Sure. Why not?" I got up so that he could sit in the seat.

Sid and I had both warned Nick that he might prefer sitting next to me, but I decided not to harp on it.

"This is a really long flight." Nick gazed out the window.

"St. Louis is a lot further away from Los Angeles than San Jose," I said.

Two minutes later, he was scrambling over me to get the airplane headphones and his Walkman that he'd left in the other seat, then crawled over me again to get into the other seat. After that, he ignored me, which was a little irritating, but I was also grateful at the same time.

Just before we landed, Sid woke up and put his contacts in. The credits on the movie were still scrolling up the screen at the front of the cabin. Sid looked a little puzzled when he realized Nick was sitting next to me. I waved at Sid to let him know that I didn't mind, and he shook his head.

Once the plane arrived at the gate, Nick wanted to hurry up the aisle and get out. I held him back. He glared at me, and I glared back. As Sid got his and Nick's carryon bags from the overhead compartment, Sid looked at me.

"What's going on with you two?"

"He's just antsy. It was a long flight for him."

While waiting for the luggage, the three of us went to the airport restrooms. Sid and I got our transmitters on, and Sid helped Nick on with his and showed him how to work it.

"Coming in," I muttered as I left the restroom.

"Hey, I heard her!" Nick said, laughing.

"I know. Stop fidgeting with your ear."

When the luggage arrived, we went straight to the car rental. It was late afternoon in St. Louis, but the first thing we did was head to the Nighty-Nite Inn on the edge of the city. It was just off the interstate highway yet was surrounded by trees and forest. A truck stop across the street seemed to be doing a lively business.

"Good location," I muttered to Sid as we pulled up on the street just outside the motel. It was a largely unremarkable boxy building, with only one story and it looked like about fifty rooms.

We had decided that I would go ahead and check things out at the desk, but that I would not do so as Special Agent Linda Devereaux unless I needed the badge to get information. One thing that Nick didn't know yet, and we were hoping he wouldn't figure it out, was that Sid and I were armed. Sid had a snubbed-nose .22 on his lower calf, another tucked into a holster at the back of his pants and covered by a linen blazer, and more hardware about his person. I had my new .357 Smith and Wesson Model Thirteen in my purse and another .22 revolver in a holster on my upper thigh, underneath the full skirt and petticoat that I was wearing, as well as plenty of other hardware in my shoes and elsewhere on my body. The guns and the hardware had been hidden from the airport scanners by the special shields we used.

Okay. The meeting, itself, was anti-climactic. I went into the office. As I asked about room rates, I dug through my purse and "just happened" to pull out the paperback version of Vonnegut's Player Piano that I'd bought the night before and laid it on the counter in front of the desk clerk. The sweet young thing looked scared, then went to get her manager. He was somewhere in his forties, balding, and otherwise not very memorable.

The manager glared at me. "You're not Player."

"No. Looking for. I've got the Breakfast of Champions." It was the code we'd been given since the Thirty-Four Alpha folks were exceptionally skittish.

In my ear, Nick giggled. "Cheetos and Dr. Pepper, Dad?"

"Sh!"

The manager tapped the book. "Not here."

"Where?" I asked.

He glared at me again.

"Code twenty-one-twelve-C gives me Need to Know."

He sighed. "Hasn't been here for months." He rubbed the back of his neck. "That whole division got compromised about a year, year and a half back. They've got a couple guys still out in the cold, but not sure what they're working on."

"How about an arms cache for sale?"

The manager shrugged. "Like I'm going to know anything?"

"If you see Player, just say that Little Red, Division Fifty-Three-Q, wants to talk."

"Sure."

I left, not at all sure that manager would do as I asked. But there was little else I could do.

"What's Little Red?" Nick's voice asked in my ear.

Sid shushed him.

The Toyota sedan that Sid had rented was still parked next to the sidewalk when I left. I turned off my transmitter.

"Well?" Sid asked as I got into the passenger seat.

"Nothing."

"Looks like we did better than you." He nodded at a small four-door car on the other side of the parking lot. "Mittman just got into it."

"Did he see us?" I asked.

"I don't think so. He came from a room at the back, and I didn't see him until you were getting into the car."

The car backed up out of the space and pulled out.

"Son, get down now!"

"Huh?"

"Down! I don't want him to see you." Sid started the engine, then pulled into the parking lot.

I heard Nick scrambling to the floor. I sighed. Convincing Nick to follow directions without asking why was going to take some doing.

Sid drove toward the check in desk as Mittman's car pulled onto the short street.

"Now, son, I want you to poke your head up and see if you can tell which way that blue car is turning."

"Uh, he's turning left, Dad."

"Alright. Sit down and get your seatbelt on."

I glanced behind and Nick was doing as he was told.

"Time to do a bit of tailing," Sid glanced my way with a small grin.

We stayed back several car lengths and almost lost Mittman a couple times, but he wasn't taking any evasionary tactics. If anything, he didn't seem to notice us.

If you're not expecting to be followed, a good tail can get pretty far. Still, it was weird that Mittman didn't spot us as he led us to a parking lot near the Gateway Arch area. Mittman pulled in and we pulled after him. Most of the visitors were leaving, it being close to five o'clock at that point, but there were a few other cars pulling in. Sid drove us to the other end of the lot.

"Want to go first?" he asked me.

"Why don't you just in case he spotted me at the motel? Give him more time to forget me."

We all got out of the car together. Sid opened the trunk and got out the SLR camera I'd packed in my carryon bag and put the strap over his head. I took Nick toward a nearby restroom as I surreptitiously turned on my transmitter, then nudged Nick. Sid went after Mittman.

"What are we doing?" Nick asked.

"Tailing that target over there."

"I don't get it. He's going that way and we're going this way."

"Exactly." I smiled at Nick. "Your dad and I are taking turns doing the tailing. You see, it's a lot easier to spot someone following you than you might think, especially if you're expecting it. To really do a good job tailing somebody, you need a whole team."

"We got one!" Nick grinned.

"Sort of. You're a little young to be walking around without an adult nearby."

"I'm not that young."

I looked at him. Already, the top of his head was even with my shoulder.

"No, you're not," I said, gazing at him fondly. "Just young enough to attract attention walking around down here by yourself. And that's what you really want to avoid when you're tailing someone."

"We're heading up Fourth," said Sid's voice.

"Come on." I touched Nick's shoulder. "We'll go this way."

We walked over one block away from the Mississippi River, turned right, then up a few more, then back toward the river. Mittman was nearing the end of the park area on the side of the street closest to the river. The arch loomed up huge and white over us. I spotted Sid almost a block behind on the other side of the street. Nick and I walked toward him. Sid spotted us with a grin. When we got to him, he gave me an improbably chaste kiss and then he hugged Nick. The three of us walked over to the river. Sid took the camera and got off a few shots, including one of Nick and me together, I later found out. Mittman was looking up the street, apparently waiting for somebody. Nick and Sid ambled away to the lower end of the park while I continued to gaze at the river. A few minutes later, Nick ran up to me and Sid was on his way around the block.

I looked up and Mittman had disappeared. "I lost him."

Nick ran up the riverside toward the top of the park.

"I got him," the boy announced in my ear. "He went up that street we came down and met Dad."

Nick came tearing back as Sid chuckled.

"Good job," I told Nick.

"Got him," Sid's voice said in my ear. "He's meeting three men, average height, dark hair, look Middle Eastern." Sid suddenly cursed. "I've been made. Operation over. Why don't you guys head to the car?"

"See you there," I said.

Sid showed up at the car at the same time we did. As we got in, feedback wailed in our ears.

"Sorry," Nick groaned. "I forgot to turn it off."

Sid laughed.

"That was fun," Nick announced.

Sid started the engine. "Yeah, it was." Sid pulled out of the parking lot and onto the downtown streets. "Excellent catch on the target, son."

"He didn't even look that way," I told Sid.

"I am so proud of you."

"Thanks, Dad."

"And I am, too," I said, grinning at him.

"Thanks, Mom."

I winced, then laughed to cover it up.

We got checked in at a hotel near the airport. Sid did his evening shave, then we went to dinner. Sid looked happy, but pensive. Nick was full of chatter about our afternoon and Sid had to shush him a couple times. In the restaurant, Nick acted out.

It was nice little steakhouse attached to the hotel where we were staying. The menu offered only a few salads and one grilled chicken dish. The rest of the menu was steaks and hamburgers. Sid has good reason to avoid red meat, fats, sugars, caffeine, and other unhealthy stuff. While he has been known to lecture when I indulge, when we're out together he doesn't usually complain. In turn, I try to back off on the really fattening stuff.

Which is why, when I ordered prime rib because I love it and almost never get it, I chose to have mixed vegetables instead of a baked potato. Sid wasn't thrilled when Nick decided he wanted a hamburger, and only put his foot down when Nick wanted macaroni salad instead of a green salad.

"You need some green vegetables," Sid told him.

"But we're on vacation," Nick protested.

"We're supposed to be, yes," I said, looking at Sid.

"That doesn't mean we can afford to over-indulge," Sid replied.

"But you did last month." Nick frowned at him, then looked at me. "He ate half a bag of Cheetos. We caught him orange-handed."

"Half the bag?" I asked, grinning.

Sid rolled his eyes. "They're addicting little suckers." He turned his gaze back on Nick. "But that was the first time I'd had any in years, and you know how lousy I felt the next morning."

"It wasn't that bad," Nick grumbled.

Sid sighed. "Maybe not, but it has been in the past. Now, I told you that I was raised by my aunt, right?"

"Yeah," said Nick.

"I used to have a really bad junk food habit. That was because my aunt was a terrible cook. We ate a lot of TV dinners, canned foods. When I was a teen-ager, I practically lived on potato chips and other snacks. Then I got a job at a fancy French restaurant and found out what truly good food is. But it was also very fattening food that wasn't very healthy, either. When I turned twenty-nine, all that bad food caught up with me. I was gaining weight. I was good about exercising, but my stomach was a mess, and worse yet, I couldn't do as much running as I used to. And one time, I got chased by a guy with a gun and almost got killed because I couldn't outrun him."

"Wow," said Nick, clearly impressed.

"I'm just lucky that Conchetta got me eating healthy. I lost weight. I was able to run again. My stomach problems mostly disappeared. I'm not joking, son. When I say your health is all you've got, I mean it. Because that's what keeps us alive. Do you understand?"

"Yes, sir."

Nick got the green salad, but he moped as he ate it, then pushed it away.

"I don't want any more," he announced.

I glared at him. "Then you don't need any French fries. Are we clear?"

"Yes, ma'am."

He did eat the salad and the moment passed.

When we got back to the double room, Sid left again to get our next flight reserved. I brushed my teeth first, then got dressed in the bathroom in a t-shirt and gym shorts for modesty's sake. Nick had gotten out a pair of plaid pajama bottoms and was wearing them. Nick went into the bathroom, came out half a minute later and I kissed him good night. Sid came in, kissed Nick good night, then kissed me, then went into the bathroom with a pair of jeans. When he emerged some minutes later, he was wearing the jeans and I was reading in bed. He was not happy as he got into bed.

"What's the matter?" I asked, putting the book aside.

"I asked you to squeeze from the bottom."

"I did." It suddenly hit me who had squeezed the middle of the tube, though. I pointed at Nick, who was asleep. "We have one more person using the toothpaste."

Sid rolled onto his back and sighed deeply. "I cannot believe I am being such a martinet about a tube of toothpaste."

He did add an expletive or two.

I looked down at him. "Reminds me of something Kathy and I talked about at camp. She said she and Jesse had been fighting about the most trivial of things, and it was really worrying her. And I said I wasn't surprised. I mean, the two of them had only been living together a few months. It takes time to get used to each other's habits. Remember how cranky we used to make each other when I first moved to your place, and we weren't even sharing a bathroom or a bedroom."

"Yeah." He chuckled at the memory. He turned thoughtful. "You know, it's almost as if we've been progressively getting more and more married since even back then."

I scratched his chin. "Three years in September."

He purred.

I frowned, even as I scratched. "I hate to be a kill joy, but you got made this afternoon. How much do you think Mittman saw?"

"It wasn't him." Sid shifted his cheek and purred some more. "A little over to the side there. Oh, yeah. It was one of the Palestinians. He looked right at me as I was coming down the street. He didn't seem to say anything to Mittman, though, and... Oh, yeah, right there. Anyway, Mittman didn't turn around or do anything to suggest that he'd seen me."

A second later, Sid caught my eye, smiled with the lecherous glint in his eyes that meant he was thinking about the two of us, well, getting involved, then pulled me down next to him.

August 22, 1985

I don't know if it was the early start or something else, but Nick was not in a good mood that next morning. It's true that neither of us are morning people, but by the time we'd eaten and gotten back to the airport, I noticed that he wasn't really talking to me. I mean, he'd answer if I spoke to him directly, but not much more than that. He also decided to sit next to Sid on the plane again, and stayed there for the whole flight, even though I had an empty seat next to me.

We landed in New Orleans around nine-thirty a.m., and had gotten wired up, a car, and onto the streets before eleven. Our first stop was at the local Nighty-Nite Inn, but the book didn't produce much from the manager behind the desk. Player Piano hadn't been there in over a year. When I got back to the car, Sid and Nick were waiting and hadn't seen anything, either.

"This is boring," Nick said, as Sid started the car again.

"That's how it goes sometimes," Sid replied.

I looked at him. I knew we needed to talk out St. Louis and now this, but with Nick around, it was not going to be easy.

We found a hotel near the airport, got a snack because both Nick and I were hungry and Sid did not want to eat at the hotel, not when the French Quarter had so many fabulous restaurants. Parking down there would be a problem, but there was a shuttle, and the hotel would be happy to get us when we called. So, we ditched the car at the airport car rental, then went off on the shuttle.

I must admit, I do love the French Quarter, although the last time Sid and I had been there had been memorable for less than pleasant reasons as well as good ones. That day, it was hot with air as thick as a pot of gumbo, and about as easy to breathe, too. We ate a late lunch on the street. Nick and I munched on beignets and po' boys. Sid found some shrimp jambalaya to go, and I could feel the spice in my nose from at least three feet away, so I had some, too. I offered some to Nick.

"No!" he snarled.

I stepped back, startled.

We found a store selling all kinds of lace, both as finished products and as yardage. Sid resigned himself and Nick almost turned surly. But I was in Heaven. I ooed over appliques, ran my fingers over silky bolts. Then I found it, a gorgeous white lace featuring tiny rosebuds among the mesh. It was silk, too, so there was a soft sheen to it and the rosebuds had a nice little bump to them.

"This is it," I gasped and dug through my purse.

Sid does not go fabric shopping with me very often, but he's been around me in enough fabric stores to know that look I get. Sighing, he slid up next to me.

"If we buy it, we have to carry it," he said softly.

"But, honey, it's my dress. It's perfect." I pulled out the pattern, which I knew I had because I'd stuck it right back in my purse after I'd shown it to him the Monday before. [And I was well past being surprised by anything you pulled out of that monster. - SEH]

He looked down at the lace, then at the drawing, and frowned trying to see it.

I flipped the envelope over and showed him the line drawings of the dress. "Here. This is the outline of the dress. Just fill it in with this lace."

He frowned again. "Yeah. It looks nice."

"I've never seen anything like it before. This is it. It's perfect. I wonder if they have enough."

My heart sank when I realized there wasn't nearly enough on the bolt for what I needed. Nick was getting really antsy, so Sid started showing him how to take pictures with the SLR that Sid was again carrying. Well, with the Model Thirteen in my purse, adding a single lens reflex camera would have been a bit much. The shopkeeper kindly informed me that the lace could be special ordered and gave me a catalog with the stock number circled. I also bought a half yard as an extra-large swatch.

"You lucked out," I told Sid as I put the catalog and swatch in my purse.

He nodded at a small table that had a deep blue tablecloth covering it with a white lace one over the blue. "What do you think about that for the table set up at the reception?"

"I really like that," I said, getting excited again. "Maybe the bridesmaid dresses, too."

Nick groaned loudly as Sid took the camera and squeezed off a shot.

I looked at Sid and laughed. "Poor thing. We're torturing him. Come on, son, we're leaving."

We did let Nick run a little ahead of us.

"So, what do we have?" I asked softly.

"Not much." Sid gazed thoughtfully at his son. "Mittman shows up at the motel, which is owned by O'Connor, then meets with several guys from the Middle East. Mittman works for O'Connor, too. At a guess, our Middle Easterners are the intended customers for the weapons stash, but that's only a guess."

"And we still don't know where the stash is, let alone who stole the weapons in the first place, if it wasn't O'Connor."

Nick came running up and pulled his dad into a store selling a host of sports memorabilia. Bourbon Street was just around the corner, but we didn't want to go there. A lot of the clubs and stores on the street are not appropriate for a boy of Nick's age. Sid did manage slip away to one of those inappropriate stores while Nick was looking at several baseball cards. At least, I figured that was what Sid had been up to when he came back with a decidedly unsaintly grin and stashed a bag in my purse. He also bought Nick a Willie Mays baseball card from sometime in the 1960s. Nick was ecstatic.

Nick did talk Sid into taking a buggy ride around the French Quarter, and then it was time for dinner. I knew why Sid had chosen the restaurant he did, and the memory of the first time we'd been there was so special. However, with Nick present, we tried to minimize the goop, as Nick usually called it. After dinner, Nick wanted to wander around the French Quarter some more, but Sid said no, it was time to go back to the hotel. Nick sulked in the shuttle.

Back in the hotel lobby, I whispered to Sid a suggestion. He nodded. I got my key out.

"Son, I want you to go upstairs to the room by yourself," I told him. "I need to talk to your father for a minute."

"No!" Nick shouted.

Shocked, both Sid and I looked at each other, then back at Nick.

"Do as she says." Sid's voice was low and measured, and trust me, you do not want to be on the receiving end of it when he gets that tone in his voice.

Nick faltered for a second, then glared at me. "I don't have to do what you say. You're not my mom."

"Oh, yes, you do!" I grabbed Nick's upper arm and marched him toward the elevators. I looked over my shoulder at Sid. "I'll page you."

Sid looked a little forlorn but nodded. I slammed the button for the elevator. As we got on, Nick looked back at his father for help and quailed when he realized was not getting any.

Poor Nick looked terrified, but I was so steamed, I didn't care. Keeping my grip on his arm, I got the door to the room open, shoved him inside, then slammed the door shut. I dropped my purse in the chair next to the door and pointed to the bed.

"Sit!"

Nick sat down, tears starting down his cheeks. "You're mad at me."

"What the hell did you think I'd be? You've only been behaving like a surly little snot all day. And that performance down in the lobby. It's bad enough talking back to me that way, but we are undercover! And you're saying I'm not your mom? What the hell were you thinking?"

Nick broke into sobs. "I'm sorry!"

My tone softened a little. "What's going on with you?"

"You don't want me."

"I keep telling you I do. Why don't you believe me?"

"I called you Mom yesterday and you made a face."

My heart broke right there. "Oh, honey. I didn't mean to. It just startled me is all." I sighed and sat down next to him. "And your dad and I have been all goopy-eyed today, too, haven't we?"

Nick nodded.

I ran my fingers through the lock of hair that had again fallen over his forehead. "My sweet, sweet guy. I want you so much. Actually, it kind of scares me sometimes."

"Why?" He looked at me sniffing.

"I don't know how to be a mom. I've never been one before. I haven't had the chance to get to know you as a baby, first, either." I shrugged. "And I am a little young to have a son your age. I was a month shy of my fifteenth birthday when you were born, you know."

"I didn't know." He thought this over. "Dad's doing okay being a dad."

"He's adjusting, too, sweetie. And you know your dad. He doesn't always let on when he's not comfortable with something. We're both trying to figure out how best to take care of you. When we should bring you with us on jobs. When we need to leave you."

Nick grabbed me by the middle and hung on. "I don't want you leaving me!"

"And I don't want you getting your butt killed." I pulled away a little and lifted his chin. "There are going to be jobs where we just can't take you with us. It's going to happen. That doesn't mean we don't want you or that we don't love you. It just means that we need to be at our best without worrying about you getting hurt. Do you understand?"

"Do you have to be spies?"

I sighed. That thought hadn't occurred to me. Henry had said he couldn't put us on Code Five status if he wanted to, and I knew Sid didn't want to be on that status. But I wondered if we could get it anyway, not that I wanted to.

"I think we do," I said, nonetheless. "It does tend to be how this business works. Once you're in it, you're in it for life. But there are compensations. You really took to tailing that guy yesterday."

"I did?"

"Yeah. You did a really good job. Your dad and I meant it when we said we were proud of you."

Nick sniffled. "Do you want to be my mom?"

I pressed my lips together. "Sweetie, if I don't want to say yes to that right now, it's because I don't want you to feel like I'm trying to take the place of your mother. She's important to you, too, and it hasn't been that long since you lost her."

"I can have two moms, can't I?"

I laughed and hugged him. "You most certainly can, young man. And, yes, I very much want to be your other mom."

"Can I call you Mom, then?"

"Yes, you can."

"Can we watch a movie tonight?"

"Let's see what your dad has to say. And speaking of…" I reached around behind Nick to the phone, dialed for an outside line, then dialed Sid's pager and punched in the code for all-clear. Sid and I had made up several codes for our pagers since we frequently used them to update each other on our whereabouts and ask questions. The all-clear code, though, came from when Sid was still sleeping around, and it let me know that any date he'd had at the house was gone.

"How much trouble do you think I'm in?" Nick asked.

"He's pretty mad. Just like I was. But..." I smiled. "I think I can give you a pass on this one. Just you never talk to me that way again. Are we clear?"

"Yes, Mom."

"You do, and I will kick your butt and you know I can."

Sid still looked pretty grim when he got to the room but lightened up when he saw me and Nick hugging.

"And...?" Sid asked.

I looked at Nick, then smiled. "It seems we had an issue or two to resolve and we did."

"Yeah, Dad." He smiled. I nudged him and he ducked his head, looking appropriately ashamed. "I'm sorry I was such a little snot today, and I'm sorry I yelled downstairs."

"Apology accepted. Don't you owe Lisa an apology?" Sid asked.

"I'm sorry," Nick said to me, and I could tell he really was. "And I promise not to talk to you that way again."

"I'm holding you to your word," I said, touching him on his chest with my forefinger. "You can be mad at me, but you cannot be rude or mean. Is that clear?"

"Yes, Mom." He looked up at his father. "Can we watch a movie, Dad?"

"It's nine-thirty," Sid grumbled. "We've got an early flight, too."

"Okay, sport," I said to Nick. "Looks like it's time for bed. Why don't you get your pajamas on in the bathroom? And squeeze the toothpaste tube from the bottom."

"Yes, Mom." Nick rolled his eyes in mock disgust. He grabbed his bottoms from the suitcase and slumped off into the bathroom.

I looked at Sid and sighed, myself. "Why do you have to schedule everything for the crack of dawn?"

"We've got a lot of ground to cover." Sid looked at the closed bathroom door. "He called you Mom."

"Yeah, that was one of the issues. He wanted to."

Sid's eyebrows rose. "Oh."

"Is that alright?"

"That's good, actually. I'm glad."

I couldn't help grinning. "So, what did you buy on Bourbon Street?"

He laughed. "So, you figured out that's where I went."

"It was pretty easy."

He came over, bent down, and gave me a kiss that was anything but chaste. "I just picked up something that I think you are going to really like."

"Ooh." I shivered a little. "When do we get to try it out?"

"Some afternoon when Nick is in school or otherwise out of the condo. The noise thing."

"How noisy is it?"

He grinned and sat down next to me, sliding his hand under my t-shirt. "I'm talking about your reaction to it."

I flushed. "I don't really scream."

"Oh, but you do." He laughed, his voice purring again. "You surely, surely do."

The next thing I knew, I had slid down onto the mattress, and we kissed, and Sid slid on top of me. We both purred.

"Bleah!" Nick screamed.

Sid rolled onto his back and laughed. "I'm sorry, son. Can I help it if I'm crazy in love with your mom?"

Nick turned down his bed, then half-smiled. "Crazy in love is okay. But you don't have to be gross about it."

He put his glasses on the night table between the two beds, then slid under the sheets.

I got up, flushing, and giggling at the same time. "Okay, we'll try not to be too gross. Goodnight, sweetheart."

I went over, sat down next to him, and gave him a warm kiss on his forehead. He kissed my cheek. Sid joined us and kissed Nick's cheek. We just stayed there for a moment.

"Dad, you look funny."

Sid glanced at me, then looked at Nick. "I'm just enjoying having my own little family."

"Yeah," said Nick. "We're a real family now." He laughed. "And not one of us has the same last name. At least, not until you guys get married."

"Not even then," I said. "I'm keeping my name."

"Cool." Nick's eyes glowed.

We hugged and kissed each other again, then I went to the bathroom to change into night clothes. Sid followed me in with his and we had to be careful not to wake Nick.

To Breanna, 6/25/00

Today's Topic: My parents' sex life

Okay. I know it was insanely embarrassing to walk in on my parents this afternoon, but it was bound to happen sometime. The reality is my parents are total horn dogs. I have never met two people who like making love with each other more than they do. I suppose between that and what happened when we went to dinner the other night, it must be pretty overwhelming.

I know you were a little freaked about how I reacted to walking in on them, and, okay, the fact that they didn't seem to care either. They do try to keep their sex life to themselves. They really do. It's just that they are crazy in love with each other, love being uninhibited, and today, they didn't know we were going to be there. And that was kind of my fault. I forgot that when they kill someone, they get hornier than normal (which is already darned horny). Mom says it's their way of doing something life-giving in the face of death.

The simple answer to your question about why I don't freak out is that I'm used to it. I mean, it's been going on since I came to live with them. They tried really hard to make sure I was asleep before doing anything, and most of the time, I was.

But then there was that night in New Orleans and Mom agreed it was time I called her Mom. She and Dad got totally goopy eyed, as I called it then. You've seen it. Dad gets that gleam in his eye and Mom flushes a little. It's only gotten worse since I was a kid. We had a double room at the hotel. Mom and Dad kissed me goodnight and, apparently, thought I was asleep. They went into the bathroom to get ready for bed and, yeah, they went at it. The worst of it was, I could hear them shushing each other so they wouldn't wake me. They really tried. The problem is, they're both screamers. Seriously, how do you tell your parents to knock it off when they're already trying to knock it off?

And it was a good thing. Yeah, it was embarrassing. I'm not going to pretend it wasn't. But you know? After what I'd been through with my first mom and the way she expected me to get used to being alone, it was reassuring that Dad and Mom loved each other so much and loved me. I hope that doesn't sound too weird to you. It's not like we're voyeurs. It's what Dad says. Sometimes what was intended to be private ends up less so, and why ruin a perfectly good hump because of it? I really hope that doesn't bother you too much.

August 23, 1985

I do tend to let Sid run the show a lot of the time. [Seriously? You also said you don't scream. - SEH] I think it's because for the first couple of years we knew each other, he was, technically, my boss. He had hired me to take care of the mundane trivialities of life, as he put it, or in other words, as his secretary. Well, that's what he'd told me initially. That it was a live-in position had to do with Quickline, but I didn't know that until after I'd been recruited. Then he was my boss in our side business because he had a lot more experience than I did.

Over time, we did more and more writing together. We officially became business partners in January this past year, which meant our assets are mingled. In terms of our side business, Sid and I act like a team most of the time. Nonetheless, if Sid wants to do something at the bleeding crack of dawn, such as running or catching a plane somewhere, no matter how much I want to throw pillows at him or sleep a few more hours, I get up and we do it.

Which meant I was mostly out of it on the early morning flight from New Orleans to Denver that next day. One good thing. Nick asked me to sit next to him, which put Sid across the aisle from us. As the plane got ready to taxi out to the runway, Sid popped his contacts out and was out cold by takeoff. Me? I just sat there staring sleepily at my book.

"Are we going to get any food on this flight?" Nick asked from the window seat.

"I'm sorry, sweetheart. I really don't know." I leaned back in my seat and tried to keep my eyes closed.

Nick sighed and I looked over at him. I could almost see him wanting to ask how late it was before Sid and I had gone to sleep the night before and not really wanting to know because the answer would be, like, really gross. In fact, Sid and I had gone to sleep at the usual time, but between the time change to Central Time and Sid's ridiculous tendency to schedule things for before when most normal humans are awake, I was a lot more sleepy than usual.

This really did not help when we pulled up at the Nighty-Nite Inn, off the interstate on the outskirts of Denver shortly after one in the afternoon.

"Want me to take it?" Sid asked as I blinked at the motel, another unremarkable box with about fifty rooms, as we sat parked in a space near the street.

"No." I yawned. "Mittman supposedly believes that Linda Devereaux is checking into this. Let's go with that."

Sid shrugged. "Okay. You just seem a little out of it."

"I am," I sighed. I looked at him and yawned again. "I am not a morning person and I do not sleep on planes."

"I know."

"I'll make it happen, love." I gave him a soft kiss then got my backside out of the rental car.

"Goop," muttered Nick.

The thing with espionage work is that it's as much about improvisation as it is planning. The manager at the Denver Nighty-Nite was an older woman with a full chin and dark gray hair cut short. She glowered at Karl Mittman as I came in. I wasn't really wearing the kind of clothes a special agent does on duty, but I did have a vest on over my nice knit top and a full skirt that almost looked professional.

Mittman smiled warily at me. "Agent Devereaux."

"How do you do, Mr. Mittman."

In my ear, I heard scuffling.

"Dad! Ow!"

"Stay down and stay quiet."

"What brings you here?" Mittman asked.

"You said you wanted to stay on top of things regarding Wade Acosta." I smiled coldly. "That trail has led here. We also heard that you're looking for somebody."

He glanced over at the manager, who, in turn, looked curiously at me.

"Yeah. Someone Wade knew."

"I see." I looked over at the manager. "I have some questions to ask, so, if you would be so good..."

"I have an interest in this," Mittman said.

"But you don't have the clearance."

"What makes you so sure?" He stepped up close to me.

I held my space. I wasn't, in fact, sure, but it would have been interesting if he did.

"The fact that you're not demonstrating that you do," I said, praying that my voice sounded calm. "Now, if you'll excuse us?"

Mittman stalked from the office. Sighing, I set my purse on the counter and began going through the pockets on the side. I pulled out what looked like a powder compact. It was, in fact, a powder compact, but with something extra - a tiny sensor that made the compact glow if a bug was transmitting anywhere nearby. I switched it on, and nothing happened, then slid the Vonnegut paperback onto the counter.

"You don't necessarily have clearance for this," the manager said as I put the bug finder back.

"Twenty-one-twelve-C, and, yes, I have the Breakfast of Champions." I pointed at the title, then nodded in the direction Mittman had gone. "Is he?"

"Yeah."

I tapped the book. "By this name?"

"Yeah."

"That's not good. He's connected to the main suspect." I tapped the book again. "Do you know where?"

The manager shook her head. "You can try South Lake Tahoe."

"Dad, that's—"

"Sh!"

"That's something," I said. "You didn't...?"

"Didn't even acknowledge that I knew Player Piano existed."

"Thanks. Let's keep it that way." I left the office with the paperback in my purse and my stomach in knots.

South Lake Tahoe was where I grew up. My parents own a resort and a souvenir store there, as well as another motel in Southern Florida, and that time of year is when they're in Tahoe. There was no way that I could pose as Special Agent Linda Devereaux and get away with it.

"We'll just have to call the Dragon and say we can't." Sid started the car and backed out of the parking space. "It doesn't do anyone any good if our covers get blown."

I began to breathe a little more easily. "That is true."

"Dad, can I get up now?"

Sid cursed. "Nick, get in your seat and get buckled in. Now."

Sid pressed the accelerator on the car and swerved at the last second to get on the Interstate out of town. Nick scrambled to do as he was told. Sid cursed again.

"Tail?" I asked.

"And he's not backing off."

I made sure my door was locked and that Nick had his seat belt on straight.

Unfortunately, that section of the Interstate took us straight into the Rocky Mountains. Sid kept pushing the car as fast as it would go, whipping around the other cars. Up ahead, dark clouds gathered, and

I thought I saw a flash of lightening. Sid muttered yet another curse, so I knew he'd seen it, too.

"Dad, what—"

"Not now! I've got to concentrate."

We were going well over ninety into mountain curves with a rainstorm on the way. I crossed myself and began praying for all I was worth. Because we were on an Interstate, the curves weren't as severe as they could have been, which was one saving grace. Also, traffic was blessedly light. Still, our portion of the road had narrowed down to two lanes. We skidded a little around the first curve, but Sid kept the car heading down the highway. Then he cursed a blue streak. A white old-style American sedan pulled up on our left side. The road began to curve to the left and there really wasn't much of anything beyond the white highway railing on the right.

The sedan drifted toward us. Metal screeched, and the steering wheel fought Sid as he steered into the sedan. The sedan backed off, but only for a minute. I swallowed. I couldn't see Nick since he was sitting directly behind me, and I couldn't turn.

The sedan pulled up again. More metal screamed and I held my breath. The last thing Sid needed was for either Nick or I to panic. The road began a curve to the right. The sedan had backed off a little. I looked over at it, since I knew Sid was focusing on the road ahead. The man behind the wheel looked as if he were from the Middle East. Raindrops pelted the windshield. Sid steered the car into the sedan and quickly backed off. The sedan went straight into the median section of the highway. Sid pushed our car ahead. The sedan had rolled over. Sid flipped the windshield wipers on, and he breathed heavily. A few miles more got us to an offramp. Sid pulled us off the Interstate, then back on in the other direction. As we slowed near where the sedan had crashed, it looked like the man had somehow survived because he was standing outside of the car. Sid swore and hit the accelerator again.

"What?" I asked.

"That was the guy that made me in St. Louis." He slipped around the increasing traffic, but at a slower pace.

We remained silent until we got to the Denver airport. When Sid stopped the car at the rental office, we collectively let our breath out.

"Dad?" Nick asked, his voice wavering. "I was really scared."

"Good. You'd be an idiot not to be." Sid took a deep breath. "But you didn't panic, and you did as you were told. That's the important thing." He turned and looked at the boy. "Do you, uh, need a fresh pair of pants?"

"No. I'm fine." His voice still squeaked with fear, though.

"Lisa?"

I took another deep breath. "I'm coming down. You?"

"Well, I don't need to change pants." Sid shook his head. "But I came damned close."

We looked at each other, then suddenly started breaking up.

"What are you guys laughing for?" Nick sounded like he was about to cry.

"We made it through again, thank you, Jesus." I crossed myself, then dabbed at my eyes, still laughing.

Sid let out a victory howl. "That was a ride for the books." He looked back at Nick. "It's okay, son. Sometimes you just have to laugh. We survived. It wasn't pretty, but we did. Any landing you walk away from is a good one."

"I don't get it."

I shifted in the seat and smiled at Nick. "It's an old joke from the early days of aviation, when planes were much more likely to crash. If you survived, that's good enough. Well, we survived."

Nick shook his head. "Okay."

Sid unbuckled his seat belt. "Alright. We need to get this car taken care of. Son, why don't you help with the luggage?" He looked at me. "How's your back?"

I gently twisted my neck. "It's fine so far."

"Let's remember to get some ice on it later tonight just in case. Why don't you go ahead and make that phone call while we deal with the car?"

"Sure."

I got out of the car rather carefully. Sid, unfortunately, had a good reason to be concerned. A year and a half before, I'd been in a car accident, believe it or not, unrelated to the spy business, and my back had gotten tetchy as a result. Working out with weights had helped, although my schedule was crazy enough that I wasn't always able to. I'd had one flare up in June, when we were moving to the condo, but had survived helping with Mae's move without one. Our ride had been pretty bumpy. Still, the muscles in my neck and shoulders, as well as my lower back didn't feel tight. I gently stretched to be sure.

I found a pay phone on the outside of the rental office, dialed the pager belonging to the Dragon, who is pretty much the head of Quickline, using the special calling card number for that purpose. I hung up and waited. Within five minutes, the pay phone rang. I picked it up, Dragon gave the caller code, I gave the receiver, then I brought her up to date on what had been happening.

"Tahoe?" the Dragon said. "Hm. That's Congressman O'Connor's district."

"There's also another little problem with it."

"Oh, that's right. South Lake Tahoe is your hometown."

"And my parents are in town."

"Well, you'll just have to work as yourselves. You've done it before."

"But there wasn't a suspect who knows me by my alter ego."

"You'll figure something out. You and Sid are good that way."

"But—"

"Lisa, you two might as well get used to working as yourselves."

"Why? What's going on?"

The Dragon laughed warmly. "You don't have Need to Know yet."

"Excuse me, but you are risking our cover, and our lives, and the lives of our son and my parents. I think I have Need to Know!"

"Oh, how is Sid's boy? I heard you two took custody."

I blinked as it finally sunk in just how weirdly the conversation was going. The Dragon had always, and I mean always, talked to us with our code names. She had never used our real names before, nor touched on any of our personal lives. That she knew our real names, where I came from, and about Nick, that didn't surprise me. That she was using our names, talking about Nick as if she knew him, that was… Beyond weird.

"Yeah. We did."

"And I hear congratulations are in order. When's the date?"

"March first." My voice was dull and flat.

"Very good. Oh, and darling. I know that we're not supposed to form attachments and friendships, but we always do. So, if there are a few people you would like to include on your guest list who might not know your real names, I think we can arrange something. And by the way, you should not interpret this as me trying wangle an invite."

I had been trying to figure out how to invite her. "Okay. Um. Bye."

I hung up, my mind spinning, and I still couldn't make sense of what had happened.

Sid and Nick were just coming out of the rental office, Nick pushing a cart that had our luggage piled on it. I looked at Sid.

"I can't wait to file the expenses on this one," he grumbled, which I took to mean that the car had cost him a pretty penny.

He, well, we are wealthy enough that we could have bought several cars without worrying about it. If Sid was feeling the gouge, it had to have been something.

He looked at me, though, and realized all was not well.

"What's wrong?" he asked.

"We're going to Tahoe."

"What? We've got a suspect who knows you as your alter ego."

"I tried making that point. She didn't buy it." I blinked back tears. "She just said we'd figure it out."

Nick looked anxiously at the two of us. "Mom? Dad? If we're going to Tahoe, that means we can't use our fake names, right?"

I swallowed. "That's right."

"But you guys say what keeps us safe is that no one knows who we are."

Sid winced. "That no one knows what we really do." He looked at Nick. "That means we're going to have to be extra careful not to say anything or even hint anything about our little side business. Are we clear?"

Nick nodded quickly.

"Especially not to my family," I said.

Nick nodded again. I think our little ride into the mountains had made quite an impression on him, and while I would have rather not exposed him to that, at that moment in time, it was a help.

We might have been able to get a direct flight to South Lake Tahoe airport, but it would have taken a couple days. The next flight to San Francisco was in a few hours, but then we were looking at staying overnight there. Still, Sid got the tickets.

"You want to rent a car in The City?" I asked. "It's only three hours to Tahoe from there."

Okay, it's technically closer to three and a half hours, but that's if you drive the speed limit.

"Might be a good idea to have our own wheels," Sid said.

So, we waited. Nick got antsy and ran around the terminal, bouncing from window to window. I told Sid the whole odd conversation I'd had with the Dragon. Sid cursed.

"You've gotta be kidding."

"I wish I was."

Sid cursed again. "We've got to get used to working as ourselves? What the hell does that mean?"

"We don't have Need to Know yet," I sneered.

Sid grumbled, but there wasn't anything we could do about it.

"It's also Congressman O'Connor's district," I said. "Which is one weird coincidence."

[And we later found out it wasn't. – SEH]

"Hm." The wheels in Sid's head were turning. "You know how a couple years ago we thought it was pretty odd that there was some activity in that area?"

"Yeah." I frowned. "You think O'Connor's part of it?"

"He is on the House Intelligence Committee, and he does get some intelligence that the rest of the committee isn't getting."

"And his aide was at the motel." I began ticking points off on my fingers. "Which, by the way, O'Connor partly owns, and then, shortly after, somebody, who could be a Palestinian national, tries to run us off the road. What does all that have to do with a missing operative and an arms cache?"

Sid sighed. "A very good question, my dearest."

"Oh, shavings! I've got to call Mama." I groaned again. "You realize the other danger we're in. We're heading straight into Wedding Central."

Sid winced. "That's okay. We've made some decisions. We'll make it work."

There was one other decision I had to make, too. Sid and I did discuss it after I'd called my mother while we were still waiting for the San Francisco flight, but he insisted that since they were my parents, I got to make the ultimate decision. He would be fine either way. Big help that was.

We left Denver shortly after three in the afternoon. The flight took less than three hours, but given the time change, that meant we landed in San Francisco around five. It took another half hour or so to collect luggage and rent the car, then we stopped on the road to eat dinner. So, we ended up at my folks' place in South Lake Tahoe a little after eight-thirty. The sun was setting as we pulled into the driveway. Mama had been waiting because even before Sid could turn off the engine, the front door to their house opened, and their two big mutts, Murbles and Richmond, came running out of the house.

I got out of the car right away and began petting my babies. Well, poor Murbles wasn't such a baby anymore. Nick hesitated, but then followed me and laughed as both the dogs sniffed him. Between their deep barks and their size, Murbles and Richmond could be seriously intimidating. Sid, however, already knew what cupcakes they really were. The dogs went running past him and got perfunctory scratches between their ears.

"Lisle!" Mama crowed. She came running down the steps and swept me into a warm hug. Daddy followed her onto the porch. He's tall and broad-shouldered and almost as stubborn as my mother. I ran up the steps and gave him a big hug.

"Good to see you, Daddy."

"Good to see you, Lisle."

You see, I was named after his mother, who is German, so while my legal name is Lisa, my parents often call me by the German version. We all got into the house, and Murbles whined a little when I didn't pet him again. I scratched him under the chin and made kissy noises, then looked up at my mother.

"Mama, he's gotten so white around the muzzle."

"Oh, sweetheart, he's ten years old. That's old for a big guy like him."

"Oh, my poor old man!" I cuddled him some more.

I'm not sure where Daddy got off to, but Mama wanted us to get settled and took us to the back of the house where the bedrooms were. My heart stopped, but I knew what I wanted and had to say.

"Mama," I said quietly, before she could tell Nick where to put our suitcases. "Sid and I will share a room."

"Oh." She stepped back and looked at Sid, then looked at me and smiled. "Well, I suppose that was inevitable. It's alright, Lisle, baby." She patted Sid's arm. "I mean that. It's perfectly alright. You two are adults." She looked at Sid again. "Only you get to tell Bill."

Sid laughed. "We'll be fine."

Sid and my daddy have had a rather difficult relationship, mostly because Daddy is really jealous of Sid. Admittedly, Sid's past behavior didn't help. But Daddy's that way about Neil, too, and Neil's father is Daddy's best friend. I really don't know what Sid told Daddy, but Daddy didn't raise a ruckus about Sid and me sleeping together.

It wasn't that late so Daddy and I got Sid, Nick, and Mama to agree to playing poker. Mama went into the kitchen to get some snacks, and Nick got mischievous.

"You know what?" he whispered loudly at my father as Daddy got the chips out and stacked on the table. "I'll bet my dad cheats."

"Nicholas!" I gasped. "Why would you say such a thing?"

"He's got that scar on his butt." Nick shrugged. "It's round, like somebody shot him."

Sid sighed and shook his head.

"You got a bullet hole in your ass?" Daddy looked at Sid.

Sid stayed focused on pulling a couple twenties from his wallet. "I'm afraid so."

"Damn," said Daddy. "Somebody beat me to it."

Sid and I broke up, then he tossed the cash on the table.

"What's so funny?" Mama asked, bringing in a big bowl of potato chips and several sodas.

"You don't want to know, Mama," I said.

We played penny ante, but Daddy and I pretty much took Sid, Nick, and Mama to the cleaners. Daddy sometimes plays in poker tournaments, and I do take after him that way. It was a lovely evening with no wedding talk.

[As for you and me in the same room, it wasn't even an issue. Your father was always far more worried about me breaking your heart than me deflowering you. I told him where we were sleeping. He asked about where we were with my AIDS tests - which was a legitimate question. I said that we were taking precautions and that was it. I do have to agree, you and your father at a poker table are damned scary. I used to think I was a decent poker player. No more. - SEH]

August 24 – 25, 1985

For all Sid and I had gotten a respite from the wedding thing the night before, I knew the second I walked into the kitchen the next morning that it was only a respite and a short one at that.

Sid had dragged Nick and me out to go running at the usual ungodly hour he prefers. I let Sid and Nick shower first, mostly because I was hoping to get something fun to eat for breakfast before Sid caught me. Instead, Mama did.

"Now, did you pick your reception site?"

I yawned. "It's in my purse. Do you have any cereal?"

"Yes. I got your Lucky Charms. Now, which place did you pick?"

"It's in my purse. Can I eat breakfast first, please?" I staggered to the cupboard and found the familiar fuchsia box.

Mama sighed. "What about your colors?"

"What about them?" I got a mixing bowl from the cupboard and a soup spoon from the drawer.

"You haven't picked them yet? Honestly, Lisa, everything we do from here on in depends on that."

"Not everything and it doesn't all have to be done now, does it?" I got the milk from the fridge.

"Oh, Lisle, why do you have to be so obtuse?"

"Because it's not even eight-thirty in the morning and I'm half asleep. Landsakes, Mama, I am not a morning person!"

Nick burst into the room. "Morning, Mom!"

"Good morning, sweetheart." I did smile and give him a cozy kiss on the cheek.

Nick's eye grew wide when he saw my cereal box. "Is that…?"

"Yes. I'll give you some." I went over and got a regular-sized cereal bowl from the other cupboard. "But the rest are mine. Are we clear?"

"Sure, Mom." He laughed as I opened the box and poured some into his bowl.

"No telling your dad, right?"

Nick sniggered.

"Lisle, should you—"

"It's a joke, Mama." I poured the rest of the box into my mixing bowl.

Nick finished his cereal in record time and dashed off.

"He's been calling you Mom." Mama sat down across from me with a worried frown on her face. "Is that wise so soon after he lost his?"

"It was his idea," I said around several spoonfuls of cereal and milk.

"Really?"

"Yeah. He said he could have two moms. I said okay. What the heck else was I going to say?"

"Oh my. It all seems so sudden."

"Tell me about it." I returned my focus to eating.

Daddy ambled into the kitchen. "Morning, Lisle."

"Morning, Daddy."

He leaned over and gave me a kiss on the top of my head. Nick wandered back into the kitchen with a pensive look on his face.

"Mr. and Mrs. Wycherly?" he asked. "If you're my mom's parents doesn't that kind of make you my grandparents?"

"What do you mean, Nick, honey?" Mama asked. "You have a grandma, don't you?"

Nick shook his head. "Not anymore. Grandma died even before my first mom did. My grandpa, he left when I was a baby. And Dad doesn't have any parents."

"Are you saying you want to call us Grandma and Grandpa?" Mama asked him.

Nick's eyes lit up. "Would you mind?"

Daddy chuckled. "I don't mind a bit."

"I don't either, sweetheart." Mama held her arms out. "Come on over and give your grandma a big old hug and kiss."

Nick obliged and I couldn't help grinning. He ran off again.

"That boy is a caution," Mama said, laughing. "Now, what colors are you thinking about, Lisle?"

I groaned. "I don't know. Navy blue."

"What kind of wedding color is that?"

Daddy grunted and hurried out of the kitchen.

"I don't want pastels," I groaned. "That is just too sick-making."

Thank God, Sid came into the kitchen at that moment. I gave him a look which I hoped said that if he even thought about talking about the wedding, I would pound him into oblivion. Mama immediately shut up about it and went to get Sid his preferred breakfast of fresh fruit, prune juice, and whole wheat toast.

Sid looked at my mixing bowl. "Is that—"

"Don't start."

Sid lifted an eyebrow and wisely backed off.

As he finished eating, Mama patted his arm.

"Now, Sid, honey, would you mind terribly if I took Lisa out this morning to try on wedding dresses?"

"Mama!"

"That's entirely up to Lisa," Sid said. "I don't make her decisions for her, Althea."

"Alright, Lisle. We'll leave around nine-thirty. I had Jean at the bridal shop put aside the most beautiful dresses."

"Mama, I don't want to go shopping for a dress."

Mama's face fell. "What?"

"I..." I looked at her and the hurt in her eyes. I looked at Sid, whose eyebrow had risen again.

"I have been waiting for so long to go shopping with you for your wedding dress." Mama sniffed.

I sighed. "Alright. We'll go."

"Very good. You be ready now." She bustled out of the kitchen.

"You're caving," Sid said.

"I know. But she was so hurt." I looked at him again. "Can we cancel?"

"Any time you want."

"Thank you."

"Oh, and remember that dress you picked?" He smiled gently at me. "That's the dress I want to see you in."

"I'm not wearing anything else."

His grin got decidedly more salacious. "I could go with that, too."

"Sid!" I shifted. "If it weren't for all the other guests, I suppose I could, too."

Sid laughed loudly, then sighed. "I love you, Lisa Wycherly."

"I love you, Sid Hackbirn." We lazily kissed. "Oh. Nick decided he wants to call my parents Grandma and Grandpa and they're on board with it."

"Good." He shook his head. "That was fast."

"Tell me about it."

"So, when are we going to look for our friend?"

I sighed. "This afternoon? Look, if I keep the peace with the gown shopping, maybe she'll let go of me long enough for us to do some checking around."

Sid went along with that but didn't seem to be holding out much hope. Truth be told, I wasn't holding out much hope, either.

"Oh, Lisle." Mama came back into the kitchen. "I meant to tell you last night and plumb forgot. Mae called the other day. She said you weren't answering your phone again."

"We were out of town," I said. "A ghost-writing thing."

That's what we'd told our family and friends the fall before when we'd had to take off to go undercover on an extended case. It was turning into an incredibly handy excuse, especially since it was a contractual thing that we couldn't talk about what we were doing.

"Well, they think they'll be moving into their new house next weekend."

"Really?" asked Sid.

"It's about time," Mama said. "The plumbing and the wiring really didn't take that long. It was that they decided to put in that extra bath for the master bedroom upstairs. Then it just didn't make sense not to repaint, then fix the floors before they got everything in there. So, they've got all new wood floors in all the common areas downstairs, and brand-new carpeting on the stairs and in all the bedrooms. And new tile in the bathrooms and kitchen. Mae says it's almost done and looks really nice."

"That's exciting," I said, then glanced at Sid. "Here's hoping our client won't have another hissy fit and we'll be able to help."

"Oh, don't worry about that, Lisle." Mama laughed. "Your daddy and I are going down there, ourselves, to help out."

I began to wish for a hissy fit from a client. "Great. Anyway, I'd better get through the shower and changed."

I must admit, trying on wedding dresses was a lot more fun than I thought it would be. The reality is when you're the bride, they pamper you, and I was surprised when I kind of enjoyed it. Not that I found a dress I liked anywhere near as well as the one I'd already picked out. They were pretty dresses, don't get me wrong. But they were awfully poufy, too. Mama had so much fun. I tried broaching the possibility of me making my dress.

"Are you out of your mind, young lady?" she snapped. "You do not want to be sewing your hem on the way to the church. Now, enough with that nonsense. What about this dress?"

I sighed and shook my head. "It's not right."

"Well, you have to like something, honey."

"Why?" I asked. "We've just started looking. There are bridal salons a lot closer to my place. Can't we check a couple more first?"

Mama smiled. "You know. You're right. Jean, honey, could you just get us the stock number on these two dresses just in case? They'd have to be ordered, anyway." Mama held up a catalog. "Now, Lisle, just look at these adorable little cocktail napkins. We can have them stamped with yours and Sid's names and the date. Won't that be cute?"

I sighed. "Exactly. Let's not."

"But we can get them in this nice powder blue."

"I don't want pastels, Mama. I hate pastels."

Mama looked at me. "Honey, what's the matter?"

"You're not listening to me. I don't want all this fuss. I don't want cocktail napkins. I just want a simple, dignified wedding."

"What's undignified about cocktail napkins?" She looked hurt again.

"Mama, I need a break." I blinked my eyes. "I want to spend some time alone with Sid this afternoon. We haven't had a lot of that lately, with Nick and all."

"Oh, dear. You haven't, have you? Alright. I have to run by the visitor's center and drop off some brochures. We'll just do that, and I'll bring you right home after that."

"Alright. Thanks."

Just dropping off some brochures for my parents' resort didn't mean handing over a stack and leaving. Mama had to say hello to the sweet high school kid interning at the desk, then talk to the center's director for several minutes. Then one of her friends came in.

"Oh, Lisle, honey, this is Marge Benson." Mama presented a short, white-haired woman with blue eyes and a handshake like iron. "Marge, this is my daughter Lisa. She's the one getting married next spring."

Marge smiled merrily. "Congratulations."

"Thank you," I said.

"Marge lives in her RV, comes in and out of town all the time."

"Sounds like fun." I smiled.

"Oh, Lisle, we ought to put Marge on the guest list. Can you believe it? My little girl is getting married in Beverly Hills." Mama giggled and dug into her purse. "In fact, I've got a picture of her fiancé and his son right here. My other daughter, Mae, took this last July and sent me a copy. It is just the cutest picture ever. There's my son-in-law, Neil, and my grandson Darby. And that's Sid and that's Nick. Isn't that boy cute as a button?"

I had to smile. It was the shot of the four guys ogling the bikini clad bottom.

"He is." Marge looked at the photo, then looked at me speculatively. "And he's Sid, you say."

"Yes. Sid Hackbirn," said Mama. "He's a perfectly lovely man."

"That's funny. I could swear I knew him as Roy Parsons several years ago. When my husband and I still had that restaurant in San Diego."

"Really?" Mama looked at me.

I shrugged, even though my heart had stopped. "Must be somebody who looks like Sid. Mama, you always say that he's a dead ringer for your high school boyfriend."

"Oh, that must be it."

"I'm sure it is." Marge handed Mama the photo and smiled at me. "But I have to say, a look like that, you don't forget too easily."

In the photo, Sid was at his sensual best, and Marge was right. That is unforgettable.

Back at the house, Mama made good on her word that Sid and I could have some time alone together. Too bad that didn't mean pleasant chatter, relaxation, and simply enjoying being in each other's company.

Instead, we drove around to Congressman O'Connor's district office, which was in a small complex of offices on the Lake Tahoe shoreline. Sid parked across the street from the door. It being Saturday, we didn't think there would be anybody there, but there was a light on, and we could see a tall, erect form pacing past the window every so often. The office was in a single-story building with rough dark-brown shingles on the roof and sides. There were a couple other offices, as well, both dark. The back of the building overlooked the lake and a small marina with a wide assortment of boats tied up, and a sea plane with bright red stripes on the side bobbing at the end of the slip.

Sid looked around at the street, then nodded at a small restaurant on the side where we were parked. It featured an outdoor deck filled with tables.

"Looks good," I said, and got out of the car.

We got a table in the back corner of the deck, where we still had a clear view of O'Connor's office and the marina behind it. Sid was wearing a polo shirt and tight jeans, and I had on a pair of jeans and an over-sized t-shirt. I'd rolled up the sleeves and knotted the bottom at my waist. We waited a few minutes to be sure, but nobody, including the wait staff at the restaurant, seemed to recognize me as a local. So, I took a chance and got a pair of small binoculars from my purse and sauntered to the street edge of the deck. It was a touristy thing to do, but it got me the information I wanted. I made it back to the table in time for the waiter to deliver a chili burger with a glass of red wine to me, and a salad and white wine to Sid.

As I tucked in, something about a chili burger niggled at the back of my mind, but it was not anything I could put my finger on. So, I told Sid about Marge Benson. He was not happy. He had, indeed, posed as Roy Parsons, waiting tables at a restaurant near the Navy installation in San Diego, trying to find out who was picking up on all the loose talk among the sailors and selling it.

"These things happen," he grumbled, then picked up his wine glass. "It's not good or comfortable, but there's nothing we can do about it except stay as far away from Marge Benson as possible. She's a harmless old lady. A bit of a busybody, but otherwise harmless. Her husband, I was a little worried about, but not her."

"Well, it also got Mama thinking about your doppelganger in Florida that she used to date. I'm sure the next time she's down there, she'll be on the hunt for your father."

"Won't do her any good. I got my features from my mother."

Sid's mother had died when he was two. His only living relative was his aunt who had raised him, and they'd been estranged since he'd been drafted into the army back in 1969.

I sighed. I'd already told him that the last thing I wanted to talk about was the wedding, not because I wanted to cut him out of it, but because I just couldn't take anymore. Mama had decided she wanted those napkins, no matter what I wanted, and wanted me to hurry up and pick my colors so that she could order them. I'd told her I'd work on the color thing as we left. Sid was not happy about that, either.

"I know you want a break from the wedding stuff," Sid said slowly. "But what's all that about the colors? I though we liked navy blue."

"Mama doesn't. It's not a wedding color."

Sid made a face. "You know, I was under the impression this was our wedding."

"Try telling her that."

Sid winced. "I have to give you points on that one."

"She's turned into a monster. I swear, she could teach Janet Weinstock a few things. And the worst of it is, if I don't like something, she gets so hurt, as if I'm judging her taste or something. She wants cocktail napkins with our names stamped on them in metallic gold."

"No. Not a good idea."

"I know. But she acted like I was ruining everything for her. That's why she wants the colors picked. So, she can order those stupid napkins."

"You could try putting her off."

I just looked at him and he sighed. Mama was in full steam ahead mode, and there was little that was likely to derail her, and we both knew it.

"Honey, she's walking all over you."

"I know."

We hung around at the restaurant as long as we reasonably could, then took a walk. The light in the office had gone off and we hadn't seen anybody going in or leaving. Sid and I shrugged and took the long way back to my parents' place.

I hung close to Sid that night out of desperation. The next morning, Nick and I went to mass with my folks, although on the way back, Mama insisted on sitting in the back seat of their Jeep with me. Not only did she badger me about the colors, she dropped another bombshell and in such a way that I could not refuse. Once back at the house, I ran for the bedroom to hide. Sid found me there a few minutes later, sobbing like crazy.

"What the hell is going on?" he asked.

"Mama. She's okay with the hotel we picked, but she wants the larger room."

"That rooms seats five hundred. I thought we were going to get a smaller one to limit the guest list."

"We need room for dancing and she's paying for it, so she's going to get what she wants. And I have to give her the napkins if I'm going to have a prayer of getting the colors we want. Only we can't have the colors we want."

"Alright. Do whatever you want. Apart from being there, I'm out of this one."

"Sid!"

"I don't care anymore. I really don't. I don't know why this is turning into such a ridiculous production, but I've had it. It's a party and a ceremony. That's it. The ceremony doesn't even mean that much." Sid raised his hands as I yelped in protest. "It's not going change our lives, Lisa. For all intents and purposes, you and I are already married. We have made our promises. Our assets are mingled. We share a bed. We have a kid. We've even seen each other use the toilet and use the same bleeping tube of toothpaste!"

[I did not say bleeping. - SEH]

"But it's our wedding."

"*Our* wedding. And right now, I'm feeling utterly indifferent about it."

I closed my eyes. "Oh, shavings. You're hurt, aren't you?"

"No. Just indifferent."

"Bull puckey. When you go indifferent, you usually care a whole heck of a lot."

He glared at me. "Well, it's not getting me very far right now. It doesn't matter what I like, or we choose. Your mother decides she doesn't like it and you cave right in."

That hurt because he was right.

"I don't know how to argue with her." I sniffed. "She's always perfectly reasonable. Or worse, gets that hurt thing going on."

"Lisa, she has your number. She knows exactly how to manipulate you, and that's what she's doing."

"She doesn't mean to be."

"So what? I'm sorry, but all this angst is not worth it to me. It's just pissing the hell out of me that you're this upset and I'm getting cut out completely."

I sniffed. "You want to be part of it?"

"Yes, I want to be part of it. It's our wedding, and I want it to be special and about us. Not what your mother wants."

"I just want to have a nice little wedding."

"Then let's have a nice little wedding. Your mother will get over it."

Nick banged on the door. "Dad? Mom? It's lunchtime."

"We've got to figure out how to tell her." I wiped my eyes.

"Let's eat lunch first."

I had to smile. I knew Sid was not looking forward to confronting my mother any more than I was. We did make one tactical error. After we were done eating, Mama talked Sid into helping Daddy and Nick clean up, then swept me off into the living room.

"Now, we do have a couple people to add to the guest list," Mama said, picking up the notebook she was keeping all the wedding details in. "Marge Benson, of course, and your cousin Maggie and Jed Simons."

"I don't want Maggie at my wedding." I said, getting angry.

"Honey, we have to. You and Sid are invited to hers and Jed's wedding."

"Then I won't go to her wedding. But I do not want Maggie Caulfield at my wedding. She's a pathetic, mean-spirited, annoying witch!"

"She's a relative."

"And you hate most of yours. And Daddy's hate you. I love you, Mama, but your families are pretty awful people. Now, I gave in on the aunts and uncles. But I am not giving in on Maggie. And don't give me that hurt look. I'm tired of it. I don't want a big, fancy wedding. I do not want cocktails napkins with our names on them. I want navy blue as one of my colors. And I want to make my own dress."

Mama started crying. "I just wanted you to have a nice wedding."

"I'm going to have a nice wedding. But it's going to be mine and Sid's wedding. Not what you think I should have because you have the money all saved up."

"You're getting a nicer wedding than Mae got."

"Thank you, Mama. You just gave her another reason to be jealous of me. And I don't want that either!"

Mama sniffed. "I only wanted to share this time with you. Mae and I got so close when we planned her wedding."

"We don't need to plan a wedding to be close, Mama."

"Mae and I didn't, either, but we got it."

"I'm not Mae!" I shrieked. "I'm me. And Sid isn't Neil. That's not saying that there's anything wrong with Mae or Neil. But I'm not her and I don't want to be. I want to be who I am. And I want my wedding, Sid's and my wedding, to reflect that. Why can't you understand that?"

Mama wept for a moment, then came over and touched my cheek. "My little tomboy." She sniffed. "You are not your sister, alright."

"You hurt Sid's feelings, you know. He wants to plan the wedding, too, and you keep cutting him out."

"Really?" Mama looked at me, puzzled. "You sure he's not just trying to be a good sport about it?"

"I'm sure. He really is interested. He's not your average man."

"Well, Lisle, you wouldn't be marrying him if he was."

I took a deep breath. "Mama, I don't want to leave you out of this, either. I understand how you feel, but I really don't want all those silly trappings. I want a sacrament. That's what's most important to me, and the only reason I'm doing this. And we're having a wedding because Sid and I want to celebrate our life and our love for each other with the people we care about and who love us. That's why I don't care about the darned relatives. They want to have conniptions, that's their problem. I know it's harder for you because you live down there half the year, but I don't see why. They're awful people."

"They are." Mama wiped her eyes. "Well, I guess I'd better go apologize to Sid." She stopped as she saw my glare. "And I'd better apologize to you, first. I'm sorry, Lisle, baby. I just got so excited." She took a deep breath. "I guess I'm still trying to make up for that awful wedding I got. The only good thing about it was that it got me married to your daddy."

"Apology accepted, Mama. I love you."

"I love you, too, baby."

We hugged, then went into the kitchen. It had been long-since cleaned and from the looks on the guys' faces, they'd heard the entire fight. Sid smiled at me proudly, then he graciously accepted Mama's apology. Mama showed him the wedding notebook and Sid's eyes lit up. He loves organizers. Mama looked up at Daddy and Nick.

"Would you guys like to help plan?" Mama asked.

"Yuck!" bellowed Nick, with Daddy's face echoing the sentiment.

"Nicholas!" I said.

"Um. No thank you, Grandma."

Daddy clapped his hand on Nick's shoulder. "Why don't we go down to the horse barn, son?"

Then Mama, Sid and I went over ground rules. We each had veto power. If something was that important to one of us, then we had to state our case. I showed Mama the dress pattern and the swatch of lace, and she was surprisingly impressed.

"I'm just worried that you'll be putting it together on the way to church."

I smiled. "I promise, Mama. I'll have it done by Christmas or I'll hire a dressmaker. Fair enough?"

"Fair enough."

We put together a list of what needed to be done and by when. Mama was also impressed that we already had our rings and happily checked that off her list. We had a bit of a tussle over the secondary color, but eventually settled on dusty rose to go with the navy blue. Sid showed her the photo of the table with the lace covering and Mama had a couple more ideas that were genuinely nice. And we got our smaller room. Mama decided that it would make passed hors d'oeuvres more affordable.

It was altogether, a perfectly lovely way to spend the afternoon and evening.

August 26 -27, 1985

Monday morning, as we went running, Nick told us that Daddy wanted to take him to the skeet range to learn how to shoot. Sid and I put him off until after breakfast so that Sid and I could discuss it.

"So, what do we do?" Sid asked in the bedroom after we'd eaten. "I don't like the idea of him getting excited about weapons."

"I don't either." I winced. "On the other hand, that's one of the ways that Daddy and I got close when I was a kid. I used to love going out to the range. And Nick does need to know how to handle guns."

Sid nodded sadly.

"Tell you what," I said. "I'll go with them. That way, you don't have to mess with it."

"Thanks."

The skeet and target shooting ranges were relatively empty considering that we were at the height of the season. Daddy signed us up for the target range first. He'd brought a shot gun and a rifle for each of us. There we showed Nick the basics of shooting, using the rifles for the targets. I'll give Nick credit. He took us seriously when we told him about the kick from the gun and, as a result, didn't land on his backside the first time he fired. Daddy watched me squeeze off a few with unabashed pride. Well, I am a dead shot. Nick had a harder time, but eventually hit the targets with reasonable consistency.

Then we went to the skeet range.

"Lisle, why don't I explain the rules while you show him how it's done?" Daddy handed me a box of shells and my old shotgun.

I got my earplugs in my ears, then got into the first position, rolled my shoulders, then mounted. Shooting skeet is not easy. I'm considered pretty good, and I've only scored a perfect round a couple times in my life. Still, I only missed three of the twenty-five shots, mostly because I was rushing the round. Daddy was smiling when I was done.

"You've still got it, Lisle," he said proudly.

"Thanks, Daddy."

Then we let Nick try, and he got twelve out of twenty-five, which is a little better than average for a novice. Daddy coached him through getting the lead on the target before squeezing the trigger, and it had worked. As we watched Daddy do his round, Nick grew pensive.

"You didn't look like you were having too much fun," he said.

"I wasn't."

"Why?"

"Because nowadays, when I shoot, I'm shooting at people, and I don't like doing that."

Nick frowned. "Is that why Dad isn't here?"

"Yes. He doesn't like it, either."

"Then why did you guys let me come?"

I sighed. "Because you're going to have to know how to use guns to stay alive."

"You mean...?"

"I sure hope not, Nick."

Daddy also noticed I wasn't as happy on the range as I'd been before.

"What's going on?" he asked when we got home. "You used to love going out to the range."

Nick had run ahead into the house.

I shrugged, trying to cover up the sadness I felt. "I know." I took a deep breath. "It's Sid. You know he was in Vietnam, right?"

"That's right."

"He hates shooting. He doesn't hate that I do it, but he did put a really different perspective on it for me. When you've heard about shooting people, even clay targets are harder to shoot."

"Well, I get that. But you got hard, honey. I don't know what to make of that."

"I'm afraid I don't know either, Daddy."

He gathered me into his arms and just held me. "You're a good woman, Lisle. Don't ever forget that."

"I'll try not to."

After lunch, Daddy talked Mama and Nick into going to see a movie. I suspect it might have had something to do with my mood. Or maybe Daddy just figured Sid and I needed some time together, which on one hand was kind of weird, because Daddy was still jealous of Sid, but really nice because Sid and I did need some time together.

As soon as we heard the Jeep pull out of the driveway, Sid pulled me into my old bedroom. Mama had put Nick in Mae's old room.

"How long do you think we have?" he asked, nuzzling my neck, even as my parents' dogs started howling.

The dogs were out in their kennel, which is why we didn't pay any attention.

I sighed happily. "At least an hour and a half."

"I can work with that."

His hands wandered deliciously, as did mine. He groaned with joy. I sighed happily.

"Oh, for Heaven's sakes!" The voice was oddly familiar but not and came from the room's doorway.

Sid and I pulled away in shock and looked. Marge Benson stood in the doorway wearing a light jacket and holding a handgun that made our Model Thirteen cannons look small in comparison. At least the automatic was pointed at the floor.

"What the hell?" yelled Sid. Okay. He didn't say hell.

Marge holstered the gun under her arm, then zipped up her jacket. "Good to see you again, Roy."

Sid cursed.

I looked at him. "Harmless old lady."

Marge glared at Sid. "He said that?"

"You're good at what you do." Sid is exceptionally good at recovery. He looked at me. "Let's talk in the living room."

Once there, Sid glared at Marge. "Okay, what division are you?"

"Several," Marge said. "But for the purposes of this case, Thirty-four-Alpha."

I looked her over. "You're Player Piano."

"Good girl." Marge smiled. "You guys are…?"

"Fifty-three-Q," said Sid.

Marge's eyebrows rose as she looked at Sid appreciatively. "You are Big Red, after all."

"You didn't figure that out?" Sid asked.

"You didn't figure out me."

Sid rolled his eyes. "It would have been nice to know."

"Probably." Marge shrugged. "I'd heard Big Red was working that case in San Diego and thought that might have been you. But the way you were chasing tail? That didn't make sense. Not usually a good way to keep your backside out of trouble."

I couldn't help giggling a little.

"I survived," Sid said. "What the hell." He waved toward the couch and Marge sat down. We landed in the two armchairs. "So, why are you here?"

"One of you has something for me."

I don't know if she caught the quick glance that Sid and I shot each other.

"Why do you need it?" Sid asked.

"Because they are map coordinates to an arms stash that needs delivering to its customers," Marge said blithely. "And only I have the map. Cat's Cradle got the stash moved, with a little support. But we have another problem, of course."

"Of course," Sid said blandly.

"The person who stole the arms in the first place, then sold them to the Palestinians."

Sid eyed her shrewdly. "Do you know who this person is?"

"You don't have Need to Know."

I was almost out of my chair before I realized that Sid was holding me back.

"Not a good answer," said Sid.

Marge shrugged. "Apparently, I don't have Need to Know, either. It's annoying, but there it is."

"So, what do you need from us besides the coordinates?" I asked.

"Not much right now. But I need you two to stay ready. I think I know where the attack will come from, so I'm gathering resources." She looked at us shrewdly. "The Dragon says you two are one hell of a team."

I looked at her. "You know the Dragon?"

Marge grinned. "I know everybody."

Sid frowned. "It's going to be tricky. We're here as ourselves and we need to keep our cover with Lisa's parents."

"I know. What a pain in the arse. You'll figure something out." She got up. "Now, those coordinates?"

I went to my old bedroom and got the piece of paper that Cat's Cradle had given me from one of the pockets in my purse. The receipt for a rum and cola and a chili burger had gotten tangled up with it, and suddenly, I was glad it had. I'd stashed the receipt in the pocket of my purse when I'd cleaned out my daypack. Not that the receipt, itself, was significant, just that it reminded me of something.

I stashed the receipt in the pocket of my jeans, then went back to the living room. Sid and Marge were laughing about something that had happened when he'd worked for her as Roy.

"You know, I really wished I could have kept you on," Marge told him. "You were good at it and the customers loved you."

Sid shrugged. "Sorry, but I was glad to be out of there. I'd already put in enough time waiting tables before that job."

I handed Marge the piece of paper with the coordinates. "Here you go."

"Thanks." Marge put the paper into her jacket pocket, then smiled at me. "By the way, do not feel obligated to invite me to the wedding. Your mother is a doll, but if she tells me one more time that you're getting married in Beverly Hills, I think I'll retch."

I rolled my eyes. "She's been a little over-excited."

Sid snorted.

"Sid!" I looked at Marge. "I think we got her calmed down last night."

"I hope so. She's been talking about putting up a display of your baby pictures at the reception."

I saw the color drain from Sid's face and felt it drain from mine.

"Ta-ta!" Marge wiggled her fingers at us and left.

"The only good thing about that idea is that I don't have any baby pictures," Sid said, gazing ahead in horror.

"I'd burn mine except Mae would kill me."

"How much time before they're back?" Sid's face still looked pained.

"About an hour, maybe forty-five minutes?"

"That thing with the baby pictures landed like a bucket of ice in my lap." He lifted my t-shirt and put his face in my breasts. "On the other hand, good odds we're not going to need that long."

I yelped happily. "No, I don't think so."

In fact, we had plenty of time to cuddle afterward, which we did after we got dressed again.

"Sid," I asked as something occurred to me. "What are we going to teach Nick about sex?"

"Hm." Sid squeezed me gently, then rolled onto his back, thinking. "I have no idea. And he's twelve. We've gotta start thinking about that."

"I know. I think we do want to be a united front, but how closely are our values that way aligning?"

"That is also a good question."

"Do you still believe in free love?"

"In principle, I do." He frowned. "At the same time, there's a lot to be said for commitment."

"Do you want him to sleep around like you did?"

"Not anymore, I don't." Sid shuddered. "Too dangerous." He looked at me. "How do you feel about him using condoms?"

"Absolutely. Are you kidding?"

"Yeah, but birth control."

I sighed. "This may shock you, but I've never been as worried about that as I quote, unquote, should be. There are plenty of good reasons to use birth control, no matter what the Church says. And, in this case, it's not birth control, it's disease prevention. That's more important."

"Alright. There's something we're aligned on."

I smiled. "And yet, you don't trust them."

"No. But they're better than nothing."

"And when are we going to tell him about our current scare?"

Sid closed his eyes and sighed deeply. "I don't want to yet, after what he just went through with his mother." He looked at me. "Maybe in October?"

"Sure."

At that moment, the dogs started barking and whining. They were still outside in their kennel. Let the Jeep pull up the driveway, and they had to let the world know how sad and lonely and abandoned they were. Mama said Richmond must have some hound in him because he had that particularly tragic way of wailing. Sid and I got up and headed to the living room. After all, there was no point in rubbing it in Daddy's nose that if his little girl was still a virgin, it was basically on the technicality that Sid and I had not been able to engage in full sexual intercourse.

I did pull the receipt from the diner in Avalon out of my back pocket and wondered if the plane that had been moored outside O'Connor's office was also the one that had taken off from the harbor in Catalina right after Cat's Cradle had been killed. I didn't get much time to think about it, though. Mama called me to help get dinner going and I shoved the receipt back into my pants.

Nick was filled with happy energy as he helped Daddy get the grill started in the back yard. After dinner, Daddy and I wanted to play poker, but for some reason, the others were not as excited about it. So, we played Monopoly. Daddy and I still cleaned up.

Sid got Nick and me up again at the usual miserable hour to go running. I didn't say anything. Sid was right, we did need to stay in shape. But I so wanted to do something about what time we ran. Later that morning, Mama proved that, while she had been chastened, she wasn't entirely unbowed.

"Honey, I just had the cutest idea," she said to me right after breakfast.

"Mama, if you have any idea that seems cute or adorable, please be warned, it's probably not going to fly."

She made a face. "I suppose Sid might not like it."

"To heck with Sid. I won't like it. I don't like cute."

She didn't quite wilt under my glare and that worried me. "Well, I suppose not."

She wandered off and I sighed. I love my mama, but the fact is, she is a force of nature and can be hard to resist. Which is why it was taking both Sid and me to keep things from getting out of hand.

Late that morning, the phone rang. Mama got it, then called me.

"It's one of your friends from high school," she said.

I tried not to give her a puzzled frown, but I was puzzled. I did have some friends who still lived in the area but had no idea who would have known that I was in town.

As it turned out, it wasn't a friend from high school. In fact, at that moment, I was hard pressed to call Marge Benson a friend.

"We need a meeting," Marge said.

"Fine. When and where?"

"Congressman O'Connor's office around one."

I frowned. "Alright."

I hung up.

"That was fast," Mama said as I came into the kitchen.

"Turned out it was nobody I actually wanted to talk to," I replied. "Where's Sid?"

He was coming in the back door. "What's up, sweetheart?"

"Can we talk in the back?"

"Sure." He smiled at me, but his face grew grim as we headed to my old bedroom.

I told him about the meeting, which did not help the look on his face. But he shrugged.

"We can't really avoid going," he said. "We'll just go wired and armed to the teeth."

I sighed.

The worst part was Nick somehow figured out that Sid and I were not going out for the fun of it.

"Nick, it's just a meeting," Sid said firmly as the two of us got ready. It didn't help that we each had strapped a pistol to our shins and had another holster in the backs of our jeans. "We'll be alright."

"Can't I go with you?" he asked.

"No. Stay here and you'll be fine."

The poor kid looked like he was about to cry, but there wasn't much we could do.

We got to the office in plenty of good time. There was a small memorial vase of flowers next to a photo of Cat's Cradle, or Wade Acosta, on the credenza in the main office, but nothing else to suggest that it was significant. Above it was a large photo of Congressman O'Connor standing next to an American flag. Sid stood stock still when he saw it.

"The congressman will see you now," said the secretary. "Right this way."

The anger wafting off Sid was practically visible, but he took my hand and followed the secretary.

O'Connor looked up as we walked in. He was a tall fellow, with broad shoulders, and reddish gray hair that was almost absent on top. He carried himself ramrod erect, as if he'd left the service, but it hadn't left him. Sure enough, there was a photo of him in his Army dress uniform on the wall of his office. Marge Benson lounged on the veranda behind him.

"Good afternoon, Corporal Hackbirn," O'Connor said.

The glare Sid turned on the congressman was nothing I wanted to be on the receiving end of.

He took a deep breath. "Colonel Landry, I have not been a member of the armed services for a good fourteen years, and you know damned well that I do not have warm fuzzy feelings about the time I spent as one."

The congressman laughed, and I don't know why he did. If Sid was calling him Colonel Landry, then the congressman should have been shaking in his shoes. I had only heard Sid mention the man a few times, and each time any number of foul epithets accompanied the mention, and that was because Landry had forced Sid into intelligence work back when Sid was in boot camp, then later made Sid continue in intelligence work after he'd gotten out of the army.

"Still insubordinate, I see." Smiling, O'Connor, or Landry, shook his head. "Even so, you've built up a pretty impressive record. Not bad for a guy who almost got himself court martialed his second week of boot camp."

"I adapted," Sid said. "You still had no right to do that to me."

"No right to do what?" O'Connor looked at him. "Save your ass from the stockade? Keep you from suffering through as just another grunt? Give your life a purpose when you got out, when all the other guys like you were getting lost?"

Sid glanced at me. "I won't say there haven't been compensations. But you also hung me out to dry several times and once set me up for target practice from the VC. And you didn't give me the option to say no."

"I liked your spirit." O'Connor shrugged. "You were a good operative even then. I knew you'd make it."

Sid cursed. "Don't try to play nice. I'm just another asset to you and always was. Now, why the hell are we here?" He nodded at the Army portrait. "I'm guessing O'Connor is your real name?"

"Yes. Career Army on the surface. If I did not get past the rank of colonel, it was because I was too valuable to the intelligence community to move higher. I served in both Korea and 'Nam."

I looked at him. "And you're on the intelligence committee because you are part of the intelligence community."

O'Connor grinned at me, then addressed Sid. "You've got a smart girl there."

"I'm not a girl." I glared at him.

[Are you kidding? That wasn't a glare. It was a demand that he spontaneously combust. - SEH]

O'Connor shifted, then smiled. "I guess not, Little Red."

I glanced at Sid. It felt weird, but I suppose I shouldn't have been surprised that he knew our code names.

"What do you want?" Sid said.

"I'm being set up."

Sid held out his hands. "And...?"

O'Connor sighed. "If I'm honest, I don't really know. It could be a political rival trying to knock me out. There's another enemy I have and it's possible he or even someone in the intelligence community wants to discredit me. Or it could be part of the scheme some of the guys in the administration are working on. They're doing something similar selling weapons to the Iranians and possibly want me to take the fall for that."

"So, what do you know?" I asked.

"That whoever stole the weapons for the Palestinians and made the deal probably also killed Wade Acosta." O'Connor shrugged. "That's who would have been most affected by having the arms shifted."

I glanced at Sid, then looked at the congressman. "Who owns that sea plane tied up out there on the marina?"

O'Connor stepped back. "My aide, Karl Mittman. He was a Navy pilot."

I smiled. "He's also your weapons thief."

Marge looked up and came in from the veranda. "What makes you so sure?"

"His sea plane took off out of Avalon Bay shortly after Wade Acosta died," I said. "I was there, so I know."

"What?" O'Connor looked shocked. "Karl? He's got no background in intelligence."

"Well, that explains a lot," said Sid. "When we were looking for Player, we spotted him at a couple of the Nighty-Nite Inns. We even tailed him in a single car, and he didn't seem to notice."

"And he was the one who wanted me to see if Wade Acosta's death was being investigated," I said.

Marge looked confused. "Wasn't that supposed to be a Special Agent Devereaux?"

My grin got a little smug. "Guess who...?"

"Damn her," O'Connor muttered.

Sid looked at him, puzzled. "Damn who?"

"Your friend the Dragon," Marge said. She looked over at the congressman.

He sighed. "Apparently, she has some plans for you two. And don't ask me what. I don't know."

Sid and I glanced at each other. The odds were barely even that he didn't.

Marge bit her thumbnail. "So, that would mean Karl is in a world of hurt. The Palestinians want their weapons, and he doesn't know where they are."

"But you do," I said.

"Wait," said Sid. "How did one man get a whole cache of weapons moved and stashed?"

"He didn't," O'Connor said. He glanced at Marge. "I have connections with the U.S. Navy, and we got a small squad of Seals to help."

I frowned. "Marge, didn't you say yesterday that the arms stash needs delivering to the customers? That would be the Palestinians, right?"

"Yes."

"Then why not just let Mittman deliver the arms?" I asked.

O'Connor winced. "He's keeping the money and he's been jerking the Palestinians around, at least that's what they've said. They couldn't tell us who they'd been dealing with though, so we've been at a loss there. We've also got an operative in Belize who seriously needs that cash." He thought for a moment. "Obviously, we need to bring Mittman in." He looked at Sid and me. "You two stand down, but don't leave town yet."

"Alright," said Sid. "If we don't hear otherwise by the end of the week, we'll assume you got your man and operation over."

We turned to go, and Sid slung his arm over my shoulder.

"Corporal," O'Connor snapped.

Sid flipped him off and kept going. "Haven't been for fourteen years. Not going back."

Somehow, I could well imagine Sid's superiors in the Army had problems with him and insubordination. I went ahead and drove back to my parents' place. Sid sat quietly as we pulled out.

"You okay?" I asked, glancing at him before changing lanes.

He made a face. "Okay enough. I could really do without working with that bastard, though."

"I'm sorry you have to deal with it."

"I may as well." Sid shrugged. "I can't change what happened, and as I said, there have been compensations."

He smiled softly and laid his hand on my knee. It was true that we wouldn't have found each other if it hadn't been for the business and Sid needing a partner.

Back at the house, we only stayed long enough to change into going out clothes. It was my idea that we needed some down time alone together and Sid's idea to go to the casinos across the state line. Nick didn't seem to mind us going out. He and Mama had rented a stack of videos and they were going watch them and eat popcorn all night. Sid and I went out and gambled and danced and later snuggled in a parking lot overlooking the lake.

To Breanna, 6/23/00

Today's Topic: The Side Business (cont.)

It was so difficult those first few weeks after my first mom died. I could tell when my parents were getting ready to go do something related to their side business. It was insanely easy. They'd get all serious, as if they were psyching themselves up for whatever they had to do. It scared the snot out of me. I couldn't help it. I was so afraid they'd leave, and I'd never see them again.

August 28 – 29, 1985

We went down to the lake side to go running the next morning, then Sid found a pay phone and called the Dragon. She confirmed that O'Connor was on the level. Reports from the Nighty-Nite Inns had also confirmed Karl Mittman checking in and looking for Player Piano, which given that his area of expertise was not necessarily on the intelligence side, was plenty suspicious. As for us, we were to stay put for the time being and just relax. Player Piano would contact us if we were needed.

"So, we're basically on vacation," Sid said as we drove back to my parents' house.

"Wow," said Nick happily. "So, what are we going to do?"

I smiled. "Well, we could go horseback riding."

"You can." Sid shook his head. "I'll stay home."

"Can we go to a show at one of the casinos?" Nick asked.

"It depends on the show," Sid said.

It all sounded wonderful and fun. Only shortly after breakfast, Sid's and my pagers went off. Nick spotted the look on our faces and almost started crying. He did wait until Mama was occupied elsewhere. Sid had taken off to find a pay phone.

"Are you guys going to leave again?" Nick asked, his voice wavering.

"We'll see," I said softly.

The news was not good when Sid got back.

"O'Connor has been kidnapped," he told me in my old bedroom. "Apparently, the idiot went to confront Mittman on his own and got bested."

"Oh, that's just ducky," I grumbled.

"It gets worse. They think they know where he's being held, and we've been tagged to go get him."

"Please tell me it's someplace nearby."

Sid shook his head. "Catalina Island."

"No!" I blinked my eyes frantically. "We can't take Nick with us."

"No, we can't."

"What are we going to do?" I paced the room wildly. "The poor kid has been freaking out ever since the page came through."

"He's going to have to deal with it."

"Sid, he's terrified that we won't come back. That we'll leave and this will be the last time he sees us."

Sid grunted and closed his eyes. "I know, Lisa. But we don't have any other option."

"Don't we?"

"What are you talking about?"

I swallowed. "Sometime before we got here, he asked if we had to be spies, and all I could think was we could go on Code Five status."

"No! That's miserably boring work."

"I know, but it's just until Nick goes to college." I blinked back tears. "That's not that far away."

Sid looked at me. "Do you really want to do that?"

"No, I don't." I looked at the door. "But I hate putting him through this. The poor thing. He's so scared and after his mother. It's just not fair to him."

"It's not fair to us, either. Do you really want to be that kind of martyr?"

I almost cursed. "Shavings! That's the problem. Martyrdom is not going to work."

"What do you mean?" Sid looked at me, puzzled.

"Remember last fall when you decided we should get married?"

"Yes."

"You didn't want to. You didn't want to make a promise to be faithful when you didn't believe you could."

"And you didn't buy it. So?" Sid watched me carefully.

"Because it would have made you the martyr. You would have ended up resenting me and our relationship would have been dead in the water."

"True."

"Do we want to do that to Nick?" I asked softly.

Sid did curse. "So, what do we do?"

"I have no idea." I looked at him. "I used to think this would be fairly straightforward. I know what my values are and what I want to share with Nick. But now that I have him, I have no idea what to do. I hate hurting him, Sid. But at the same time, I don't want to give up who I am. I can't see that being good for him."

"It's not." Sid began pacing, as well. "On the other hand, is it fair to traumatize him this way?" He looked at me. "What do we do?"

"I have no idea." I took a deep breath. "I remember you saying that giving up sleeping around was actually pretty easy."

"Yeah. So?"

"It was because by then, you wanted to."

Sid thought. "Yeah."

"So, any sacrifice we make for Nick should be because we want to. Because we think it's worth it."

Sid nodded. "Okay. How does that help us here?"

I smiled at him. "How badly do you want to go after Mittman?"

"How badly?" Sid laughed. "I want to take him down but good."

"So do I." I sighed. "That's kind of the problem. How do we explain that to Nick in a way that reassures him and still gives us room to be who we are?"

Sid smiled. "We remind him who we are."

"I think so." I closed my eyes. "Sid, what did Dr. Heilland say? That kids are resilient. If we surround Nick with love, he'll be okay."

"That makes sense."

"My parents love him."

"They do."

I smiled wanly. "Then we'll count on that."

Sid sighed. "I'll go get him."

Nick was not ready to give in that easily.

"Why do you have to go away?" he cried, sitting on the edge of the bed. "I don't want to lose you!"

"We don't want to lose you, either, Nick," Sid said. "But there are going to be times when we have a job to do, and we can't take you with us."

"Why do you have to be spies?" He began weeping.

"Because that's who we are," Sid said calmly. "It wasn't what Lisa or I chose. It was what happened, and we went with it. We had no idea you even existed at that point, and by the time we did know about you, we were already there." He sat down next to him. "I know. It sucks. The problem is, Lisa and I like what we do. There are parts we don't like. Being afraid."

"I don't like that," I said.

"Putting you in danger."

"I really hate that part," I said.

"But it's all part of what we do." Sid squeezed Nick's shoulders. "We didn't want to pull you into it or put you in the position of constantly worrying about us. That was why it was so damned hard to take custody of you. We didn't want you to have to deal with all that." He sighed. "But we wanted you, Nick. We love you and you're a great kid and you make me so damned proud."

I slid up next to the boy and held him, too. "Nick, sweetie, we can't promise we're coming back. We couldn't if we had boring jobs that didn't involve bad guys shooting at us. Your mom wasn't supposed to die of leukemia, and yet she did. These things happen, and they're awful. But I promised you that I would not leave you alone, and you will not be alone. Nick, there are a whole bunch of people who love you almost as much as your father and I do. And they will take care of you. I've already asked them to, so I know they will. Your Aunt Mae and Uncle Neil will be there if your dad and I can't be. They've already said so."

"But I want you guys," Nick cried.

"I'd rather be here, too," Sid said. "And I like the odds that Lisa and I will be. We just can't promise is all."

"And knowing that," I said. "We made sure that you will be taken care of. Nick, that's the best we could do even if we had boring jobs."

"I'm just so scared," he said.

I pulled him close and kissed the wavy dark hair so much like his father's. "I know, baby. I get scared, too. But we just have to face it. And remember, my darling, your dad and I are in God's hands. I trust in that, and I know it's hard to when you've already lost your mom and your grandma. But I do know that no matter how bad it gets, there is always some blessing in it. I really do believe that, my sweet guy."

Nick broke down in sobs and Sid and I held him for quite some time.

We eventually had to turn him over to Mama and Daddy.

"He's grieving," I told Mama. "And he's scared that he won't see us again. That's what he told us when his mom was in the hospital. That he'd leave and never see her again, and it happened."

Mama sniffed. "Oh, that poor little angel. Lisle, do you and Sid have to go?"

"I'm afraid so, Mama." I shrugged. "He's going to have to get used to it at some point and the more we delay it, the worse it's going to get."

Mama sighed. "You're right about that. Oh, dear. I'd better go make some cookies."

I smiled. I remembered when warm, fresh out of the oven cookies and my Mama's hugs could soothe anything. Sadly, even the worst of my heartbreaks were nothing compared to what Nick was dealing with. I closed my eyes and sighed.

Neither Sid nor I were in a particularly good mood as we packed our suitcases. We got to the Tahoe airport by one in the afternoon and just barely caught a flight to Long Beach, then made a quick pick up. From there, we caught the last boat to Catalina, again by seconds.

"How are you feeling?" I asked Sid as we watched dolphins playing in the wake of the boat.

He shrugged. "I'm trying not to. You know, it really sucks having to leave Nick like that. But it's going to be inevitable."

"I know. I can't help wondering if we're really being good parents."

"We're doing the best we can. According to both Neil and your dad, that's pretty much all you can do."

"So, I've heard." I leaned next to him.

When we got to Avalon, Sid went ahead and got us a hotel room, while I picked up a few extra tools we might need. The pickup in Long Beach had been for some more deadly equipment. Once in our room, Sid and I went over our operation.

Surveillance had pinned Mittman's location down to a cove about midway around the island. It was pretty much a perfect set up from Mittman's point of view. There was no way anyone could approach by either sea or air without Mittman spotting them. Walking in was pushing it. I looked at the trail map and really focused on landmarks that I already knew. I'd walked between the church camp and Avalon three times before. Beyond that, I was a little unsure. On the other hand, I'd done a fair amount of hiking in my life, so trail maps were not the cipher they were to Sid. I did make sure we had plenty of water for our day packs along with the rope, crampons, and the high-powered rifle and ammo.

The sun hadn't quite risen when Sid and I got on the trail that next morning. Once we crested the hills that rose up from the ocean, it wasn't that bad a walk. I pointed out the church camp as we walked along the ridge that hovered over it.

"That's it?" Sid asked peering down into the little delta at the rough cabins and outhouses. "Good gravy, woman, please tell me I will never have to go there."

"It's just rustic," I said with an amiable grin.

We were wired. We knew at some point that we'd have to call for support, although we had no idea what form that support would take. I had forgotten, however, that my transmitter was on. We kept walking.

"Honey," I asked somewhere over the next cove. "I just had an idea. About our son."

"Oh?"

"What if I adopted him?"

"Do you want to?"

"Yeah, I do. I think it will give him some extra stability. Besides, if you bite it and I don't, it will make it easier for me to take care of him."

"It might at that. I'll call the lawyer as soon as we're done here." He paused. "We'll have to see what the boy says, though."

"Of course."

It was easy to spot the cove where Mittman had holed up. The sea plane with the red stripes bobbed in the tiny bay. A rustic cabin sat next to the hill rising above the delta that opened onto the sea. Sid and I flattened ourselves against the ridge over the opposing hill to the cabin. Sid got the binoculars out of his day pack and searched the cove.

"I think I see him in the cabin," Sid muttered. "No sign of O'Connor, though."

"Odds O'Connor is still alive?" I asked.

Sid swore. "Damned good. Mittman's pushing him outside to the landside of the cabin."

I looked and saw the two tiny figures below. "No outhouses and I'm willing to bet no plumbing, either."

Sid shrugged, but we both skirted around the cove to the other hill. Mittman was still standing over a bound and blindfolded O'Connor. I got into my day pack and pulled out the rectangular box inside. My stomach knotted a little as I assembled the high-powered rifle, but that was the plan. Sid whacked a couple crampons into place next to a boulder, just as I'd told him how.

"You okay?" I asked.

He shrugged. "Not my idea of a good time, but we need you up here with the rifle."

He was right. I was the better sniper of the two of us. I handed him the rope I'd had looped over my head and across my body, and he tied it to the crampon.

"You ready?" He asked after pulling on some gloves and looping the rope around his hand.

"Yep."

"Commence fire."

I aimed and landed a shot next to Mittman's right foot. He swore and looked around. I put several shots around him and managed to push him away from O'Connor. It took several more shots, but Mittman had backed up a good hundred yards from the congressman. Sid used the rope to climb down the hill. Anytime Mittman tried to advance on O'Connor and Sid, I shot the sand near the aide's feet, and he bounced back. Technically, I probably should have just killed Mittman, but that was not something I could do. Sid got O'Connor free of the handcuffs and blindfold. O'Connor got sent up the hill first. He was a little surprised to see me laying on my tummy and firing at Mittman, but I didn't say anything. O'Connor sent the rope down after Sid almost immediately. When Sid was about to crest the hill, I got up and went to pull him up the rest of the way. Except the edge gave way. I slid down several feet, only stopping myself by grabbing onto a shrub of some sort. O'Connor finished pulling Sid up, and Sid reached down to me.

Mittman, in the meantime, ran to the cabin and emerged with his own rifle. I got Sid's hand just in time to feel the whiz of a bullet flying past my head. Sid and O'Connor both swore, but O'Connor was able to grab my rifle and started shooting. We had to stay low as we skirted the cove back toward Avalon.

"Air support!" Sid hollered. "We have the extraction. We need out of here now!"

We ran down the trail, all too aware of the sound of the sea plane starting up. That, however, was drowned out by a helicopter that hovered over us, then set down on a small plateau nearby.

We ran. Sid and the congressman got into the back seats. I landed in the front seat next to Marge Benson, who was piloting the chopper.

She shot a thumb at the helmet behind me. I saw Sid and O'Connor grabbing similar next to them. I strapped in, then put the helmet on.

Benson already had us in the air. I felt rather good about it until I realized that the sea plane was in the air and coming at us.

"Incoming at three o'clock," Sid hollered through the radio in the helmet.

"Got it," Marge hollered back.

The chopper sank with a sickening drop, then rose and flew faster over the island. I saw the sea plane rise, then dive right at us again. Marge pulled the chopper up and away. In front of us, the Avalon airport grew nearer, but I wondered if it would be near enough. A minute later, the sea plane dove at us again, then all the world was spinning.

"Brace!" yelled Marge's voice. "We're going down!"

"Hail Mary, full of grace, the Lord is with you," I muttered frantically. "Blessed are you and blessed is the fruit of your womb, Jesus."

The noise was tremendous, but in the aftermath, the sea plane's roar faded. The shock of the impact jarred every bone in my body and nearly knocked me out. My lower back exploded with pain.

"Evacuate," called Marge's voice. "But stay down."

I got out of the belts and ripped the helmet from my head. Behind me, Sid was doing the same. The chopper's main rotor blades whirled slowly above us as we peeled away from the wreck. We stayed low. Marge and O'Connor ran in the other direction, but I could hear Marge's cackle above the whir of the rotor blades and the sirens approaching us. Sid grimaced as he bent over his right hand.

I reached out to him. "You okay?"

"My wrist," he grunted. "You're bleeding."

My right temple throbbed and when I touched it, it was wet. The blood stained my fingers. I held Sid close, my lower back screaming in agony.

"Honey," he gasped. "If you can make this God thing work, could you see to it that I never have to get on another helicopter again?"

I chuckled blankly. "I'll do what I can, my love."

August 30 – September 7, 1985

We spent most of the night in the hospital. Sid and I had the worst injuries, but neither were as serious as those of a group of partygoers whose boat had caught fire. Marge and O'Connor, who both had a nice assortment of cuts and bruises, waited with us in the waiting room. Sid had an ice pack on his wrist, and I had another on my lower back. My cut had been bandaged, but nothing more. I did make a point of calling Nick as soon as we knew we'd be waiting to let him know we were mostly okay. As I hung up the pay phone, I noticed O'Connor looking at us.

I sat back down next to Sid and adjusted the ice pack on my back. "How are you feeling?"

"I'll live."

O'Connor settled in a row of seats across from us. "What's your status with the kid?"

"What?" I asked.

"According to the Dragon, you just took custody of a kid."

"My son," said Sid, giving him the evil eye. "His mother passed at the beginning of the month."

"And you want to adopt." O'Connor pointed at me.

"What?" Sid and I both said.

"You were wired. Marge heard and told me."

Sid cursed. "That's right."

"According to California law, you'll have to wait until you're married to file the petition," O'Connor said. "Although…"

"We're getting married in March," I said, my heart sinking.

O'Connor shrugged. "I could make it happen faster."

"Why?" asked Sid.

"The kid needs stability."

Sid looked at him cynically. "You're not that altruistic."

"Hell, no." O'Connor laughed. "But you two are good operatives. I can't have you distracted by worrying about your kid. When do you want it to go through?"

"By the end of the year," Sid said.

O'Connor frowned. "We could try. But I can definitely make it happen before March. Just do me a favor and make sure the kid is up for it. I'll have the attorney call you next week. Get the paperwork filed just like she says. I'll take care of the judge." He made a note on a piece of paper he had in his hands.

"Why?" Sid asked again.

"Like I said. You're good. I can't have you distracted." O'Connor smiled, then looked away for a second. "And maybe I'm trying to make up a little. You were right, Sid. I did leave you hung out to dry a couple times. Not because I wanted to, by the way. I just liked your odds better than my other options." He gazed down at the floor. "Funny how your perspective changes as you get older. Back then, you reminded me a lot of myself at that age. Cocksure and using that bravado to cover how scared and lost I was. The military saved me, and I was hoping it would do the same for you. When I saw you on that bender when you got discharged, I got worried. I could see what was happening to too many of our boys, and you'd seen worse than a lot of them. That's why I roped you back in."

Sid pressed his lips together. "I still resent that you didn't give me a choice."

"No. I gave you a choice between being court martialed or accepting my offer."

"Wow. What a great alternative."

"You should have kept your pants zipped, son."

Sid sighed and the hint of a smile played on his lips.

They called me back to the treatment area first. Apparently, there was a time issue with getting my cut sewn up. By the time I was done, Sid was in x-ray. Another hour later, his right wrist was in a cast, and we were put out on the deserted streets of Avalon. Marge drove us to the hotel, where we almost didn't get undressed before we were asleep. Marge was somehow waiting for us when we got up the next morning. We checked out and headed for the bay and the boat service back to the mainland. As we walked on the quay, I saw Mittman's sea plane bobbing in the harbor.

"Why's he still here?" I asked, my heart in my throat.

"He spent the night at the safe house." Marge smiled smugly. "In the meantime, the congressman was able to request some help. Mittman won't get very far, and the money is already on its way to Belize."

A minute later, the sea plane powered up. It turned around in the bay, then took off, rising into the blue sky of the early morning. The bright orange of flames and black smoke suddenly consumed the plane, then we heard the bang.

"I love Navy Seals," Marge said, as my stomach turned.

Sid and I got tickets for the next boat back to the mainland, then I made another couple calls, including one to my parents.

"They were planning on flying down anyway," I told Sid as we got onto the boat, dragging both my suitcase and his. His right arm was in a sling, but he had both our carry-ons slung over his left shoulder. "We'll have enough time to get back to the condo, get changed and get out to the Burbank airport before they arrive."

"We don't have to rush home."

"Yeah, we do. Our boy needs to see us."

Sid smiled and squeezed my hand with his good one.

We took a cab back to the condo. I couldn't believe Sid had enough cash on him to pay for the trip, but he did. It didn't take long to change clothes, then I drove us out to Burbank. We did get there about half an hour early. As the passengers from the plane from Tahoe filed into the gate area, I watched anxiously. I spotted Daddy first, which was easy to do since Daddy is pretty tall. Nick burst through that pack into Sid's and my arms. He bounced back when he saw the cast on Sid's arm.

"Dad, are you okay?"

"Just a hairline fracture," Sid said, holding Nick with his left arm.

"Mom, what's that bandage?"

"Just a cut."

"Landsakes, Lisle," said Mama coming up. "What on earth happened to the two of you?"

"We were in a little accident," Sid said with a smile. "Any landing you walk away from, right?"

Nick laughed as my parents sighed.

Mama shook her head. "The way you two drive, I'm surprised it doesn't happen more often."

The next day was filled with utter chaos. The movers were at Mae and Neil's new place, which still needed considerable work, but was at least habitable. They had the contractors coming the next week to put the new roof on. A couple of the outside doors had dry rot and would need to be replaced. Every room needed new curtains. The utility room at the back of the kitchen was too small for both the washer and dryer. The kitchen had relatively new appliances, but the plywood cabinets needed replacing. Mae was everywhere, trying to make sure everything was perfect and there was no way it could be.

I was still walking a little crooked from my back pain, which had just barely backed off. Sid did a surprising amount of unpacking with only one hand. Nick was into everything. Mama and Daddy stayed at the new place, while Sid, Nick, and I drove back and forth from Beverly

Hills to Pasadena each day of the weekend, which included Monday, Labor Day.

That evening, as we drove home, we told Nick that I wanted to adopt him.

"Okay. What's that mean?" he asked.

"It means I'll officially be one of your parents," I told him. "That way, if something happens to your dad, I'm automatically in charge. We don't have to worry about wills or anything else."

"You mean you'll be my mom?"

"Legally, yeah."

The car echoed with the whoop of Nick's joy.

First thing that morning I was finally able to order the lace for my wedding dress. The woman at the store in New Orleans assured me that she'd be able to get enough of the lace, and I even paid for overnight delivery.

Amy Wetterling, the adoption attorney, called right after and set us up to visit that afternoon. Wetterling informed us that since it was a stepparent adoption and since Nick's mother was deceased, it would be as straightforward a process as could be, even though Sid and I weren't married yet. The judge had already been arranged and was, apparently, not worried about when the wedding was going to happen.

The next day, I found in the mail something I'd asked Marlou Parks for. That sent me on an errand. I found what I wanted quickly but waited until I kissed Nick goodnight to give it to him.

"What's this?" he asked, sitting up against the rail on the top bunk of his bunk bed.

"A double picture frame. Open it."

He did and started crying. "It's my moms."

I went up the ladder and sat next to him. One side of the frame held a photo of Rachel and Nick together, Rachel's head swathed in a bright-colored scarf. The other held the picture of Nick and me together near the Gateway Arch that Sid had taken a couple weeks before.

"Your first mom is just as important as I am," I told him. "And I am very glad to be your second mom."

Wordlessly, we held each other.

To Breanna, 6/23/00

Today's Topic: About the Picture.

I was so glad when you found that double frame. I know. I freaked out about it. And you were right that it had simply been misplaced in the move to my new place. But the pictures inside are incredibly important. That frame has been on my bedside table since Mom Two gave it to me.

You know how the night we decided to start dating I told you that the whole business of one month and done was about finding the person that fit? I was at the done point with Kristen the night of my birthday party last February. But that's also when it hit me about you.

Kristen didn't mesh. You did. Kristen didn't want to sing along. You did and played blues guitar and let Dad follow you on my keyboard. Kristen thought Josh was ridiculous. You thought he was hysterical and got that he was just being silly. Kristen hated classical music and didn't want to go to the concert. You were already a fan and had the CD.

I know you thought I was pretty harsh when I broke it off with Kristen the next night. Like I told you, I didn't really have much choice. I usually let my girlfriends end things on their own, but Kristen, she wasn't getting the hint. She'd come over for Valentine's Day and had forgotten that's my actual birthday. Worse yet, she brought over that really crappy pizza from that chain place you and I hate so much.

So, I shut down. It was not going to work, and I knew it. Well, she decided it was time to have sex and went right into my bedroom and started looking around and found the frame. She asked about Mom One, and I explained that she was my first mom and that she'd died (never mind that I'd already told her about that). She closed the frame, put it back on the bedside table, and said that she thought it was morbid to keep a picture of a dead person out.

Then she tried to undress me. I said no. And she said we were having sex, or we were not going to be together. I said good-bye and showed her the door.

So, when you found the double frame today, I was insanely grateful. But I also had to hold my breath. Would you understand? And you did. You have no idea what that means to me.

Mom Two gave me the picture a couple days after she and Dad told me that she wanted to adopt me. She did worry that I would think that she was trying to take my first mom's place, which is why she included a picture of my first mom and me in the frame. When Mom told me that my first mom was just as important as she was, I knew then just how fiercely she loved me. And I loved her so much.

You talk about the wall my parents and I have built around us. That was the side business, but it's made us incredibly close. That Mom invited you into the compound, such as it is, is still a shock to me, but one I am so glad for.

Over the next few evenings, I laid out and cut the wedding dress from a piece of old sheet. It sewed together quickly, but that Saturday, I had a problem. Nick was over at Kathy and Jesse's doing something. Sid came into the condo and found me in the bedroom, struggling to get the back seam in the dress pinned while I was wearing it.

"Oh, peewaddles!" I groaned.

Sid laughed, then looked at me curiously. "It looks like you've got that on inside out."

"That's so I can make adjustments," I said. "Ow!"

"What?"

"I just poked myself with a pin." I said, reaching behind myself again.

Sid sighed. "Okay, you need to close up that back, right?"

"Yeah. It's just hard to stick the pins in vertically while I'm wearing it."

"I can do that."

"You want to?"

"Sure. Why not?"

"No reason."

It took a couple minutes of coaching as I watched what Sid did in the closet mirror, but he did get it. I looked at the front critically.

"What now?"

"I have to figure out where my bust points are to be sure the darts line up correctly."

"Darts?"

I waved one of the small flaps of fabric that had been folded into a triangle, then got a red felt-tip pen off the dresser.

"I have to make darts to make the fabric fit over my curves," I explained. "Fabric is essentially two-dimensional, and darts make it three-dimensional."

Sid took the pen with his left hand, then reached his finger out. "Let me guess. That's one bust point."

I hissed with the pleasure. "Yes."

"Okay. Let's mark it." He drew a little circle around where my nipple was underneath the dress and my bra, then made a happy face out of it. "And this should be the other one."

I giggled as he repeated the procedure. "You're being silly."

"Why not?" He pulled the fabric at the back seam. "Can you move your arms okay?"

I did. "Yeah. Looks like I've got it. Can you draw lines on either side of the pins, please?"

"Okay." The felt tip pin slid down the center of my back. "So why do it this way?"

"I'm not cutting into that beautiful lace until I'm sure the pattern fits."

He smiled and looked at me again. "Maybe I should mark this from the inside."

"Sid, the bedroom door is open."

I heard it shut.

"No, it's not." He lifted my skirt and slid underneath.

"Sid…" I gasped as he gently kissed the insides of my thighs. "Sid!"

Okay. I screamed.

Coming Soon

Book Nine in the Operation Quickline series *Just Because You're Paranoid*

It doesn't mean they're not out to get you

First, there's the wedding. Not Sid and Lisa's, but her cousin Maggie's, where Sid and his son, Nick, raise all sorts of eyebrows.

Then there's the attempt on Sid's life. Then Sid and Lisa's good friends are recruited into their top secret organization. Then there's Lisa's sister being jealous, a new house getting close to being ready, Sid and Lisa's own wedding to work on, plus Nick bringing home every bug there is at his new school and sharing it with his parents.

The circles of family complications ripple outward as Sid and Lisa try to cope while training their two friends and staying ahead of a ruthless killer determined to take both of them out.

Other books by Anne Louise Bannon

I'm so glad you liked this book! Check out my other novels, available in print or ebook at your favorite retailer:

Freddie and Kathy Series:
Fascinating Rhythm

Bring Into Bondage

The Last Witnesses

Blood Red

Operation Quickline Series
That Old Cloak and Dagger Routine

Stopleak

Deceptive Appearances

Fugue in a Minor Key

Sad Lisa

These Hallowed Halls

My Sweet Lisa

A Little Family Business

Old Los Angeles
Death of the Zanjero

Death of the City Marshal
Death of the Chinese Field Hands
Death of an Heiress

Daria Barnes
Rage Issues

Mrs. Sperling
A Nose for a Niedeman

Brenda Finnegan
Tyger, Tyger

Romantic Fiction
White House Rhapsody, Book One and Two

Fantasy and Science Fiction
A Ring for a Second Chance
But World Enough and Time

And I would be honored if you left a review for this and any of my books on GoodReads or any other retail site. It really helps.

Connect with Anne Louise Bannon

Thank you for sticking it out this long! Please join my newsletter. It's the best way to stay up-to-date on my upcoming projects, blog posts and even games and giveaways.

Sign up here: http://eepurl.com/zH0Ab

Or connect with me on your favorite social media platforms:

Visit my website: http://annelouisebannon.com

Friend me on Facebook: http://facebook.com/RobinGoodfellowEnt

Follow me on Twitter: http://twitter.com/ALBannon

Favorite my Smashwords author page: https://www.smashwords.com/profile/view/MsBriscow

Connect on LinkedIn: http://www.linkedin.com/in/annelouisebannon

Follow me on Pinterest: http://pinterest.com/msbriscow

About Anne Louise Bannon

Anne Louise Bannon is an author and journalist who wrote her first novel at age 15. Her journalistic work has appeared in Ladies' Home Journal, the Los Angeles Times, Wines and Vines, and in newspapers across the country. She was a TV critic for over 10 years, founded the YourFamilyViewer blog, and created the OddBallGrape.com wine education blog with her husband, Michael Holland. She is the co-author of Howdunit: Book of Poisons, with Serita Stevens, as well as author of the Freddie and Kathy mystery series, set in the 1920s, the Old Los Angeles series, set in 1870, and the Operation Quickline series, plus several stand alones. She and her husband live in Southern California with an assortment of critters.